ABOUT THE AUTHOR

When Chris Behrsin isn't out exploring the world, he's behind a keyboard writing tales of dragons and magical lands. Born into the genre through a steady diet of Terry Pratchett, his fiction fuses a love for fantasy and whimsical plots with philosophy and voyages into the worlds of dreams.

You can learn more about his fiction and download two free books at his website, chrisbehrsin.com.

facebook.com/chrisbehrsin

x.com/chrisbehrsin

goodreads.com/cbehrsin

bookbub.com/authors/chris-behrsin

BOOKS BY CHRIS BEHRSIN

DRAGONCAT SERIES

A Cat's Guide to Bonding with Dragons

A Cat's Guide to Meddling with Magic

A Cat's Guide to Saving the Kingdom

A Cat's Guide to Questing for Treasure

A Cat's Guide to Travelling through Portals

A Cat's Guide to Vanquishing Evil

A Cat's Guide to Dreaming of Fairies

A Cat's Guide to Dealing with Destiny

A Cat's Guide to Preventing Oblivion

A Cat's Guide to Serving a Warlock (Prequel Novella)

SECICAO BLIGHT SERIES

Sukina's Story (Prequel Novel)

Dragonseer

Dragonseers and Bloodlines

Dragonseers and Automatons

Dragonseers and Evolution

More works available at: https://chrisbehrsin.com

DRAGONCAT BOOK 9

A CAT'S GUIDE TO PREVENTING OBLIVION

CHRIS BEHRSIN

WORLD WALKERS PUBLISHING

Copyediting by Tarryn Thomas
Cover Design Layout by Chris Behrsin

ISBN: 978-1-915886-59-0 (paperback)
ISBN: 978-1-915886-58-3 (hardcover)
ISBN: 978-1-915886-56-9 (e-book)

Published by Worldwalkers Publishing Ltd

For cats and for dragons

PROLOGUE

CANA DEI

They say that history always repeats itself, that time by its very nature is just a series of cycles, with the same stories occurring again and again. As one cycle ebbs another emerges, and so the temporal dynamo spins, never ceasing. If it's happened once it's practically destined to happen again. Thus the sun will always rise tomorrow, and night will always fall soon after. There can never be an end to it all.

But no creature in any of the dimensions has lived long enough to truly understand its essence. No one can quite remember their beginning, and so no one can fully comprehend how it all must ultimately end.

They call me the dark force, and I have many names, but you probably know me as *Cana Dei*. It is I who shall end it all, who'll return nature to the darkness from which it emerged. It is I who shall break the cyclical nature of existence and transform it back to its inevitable state.

You might call it destiny, or the more fearful amongst you might use the word oblivion. This is how it must ultimately end.

As dawn breaks over our battleground to be, namely the First Dimension, the world spins and the darkness that has plagued a cold and bitter winter lifts its mantle to make way for spring. False spring, it should be called, because each sprouted sapling and blossoming flower brings a kind of hope that cannot ultimately be realised.

Eventually, everything must wilt.

Warlocks of the First Dimension, your time will soon come. You have been largely silent since you turned upon your master Lasinta because she refused to bend to my will. Now you answer only to my commands, but I assure you that you've made the right choice.

Seramina – the one who betrayed us – might have destroyed your original army. But time has passed, and under my tutelage you have raised a magical horde that rivals any force your world has known. Not to mention the demons that you shall soon summon from the Seventh Dimension, brought forth from the rifts that you will break into the ground itself with the spell that we have nearly perfected.

Of course, there are those who are destined to protect the First Dimension. The King's Dragon Guard on their powerful dragons trained by the mighty Matharon himself; the White Mages on their unicorns, who police the lands against those that might 'fall' to the darkness. Then there's the cats who have learned to ride dragons. They seem laughable when you think about it, but that won't stop them from emerging as one of the most powerful forces the worlds have ever seen.

Alas, none of them will be powerful enough – because I have the warlocks, I have the demon overlord Ammit, and I have others who will eventually serve me in the future, including the traitor who is yet to be revealed.

As for the rest of you, well, let's just say that your preordained oblivion is nigh . . .

CATS IN TRAINING

It was a strange thing, and I'd never thought I'd ever say it, but I was starting to enjoy the cold. It howled around me, announcing its fury in the form of winds buffeting against those who resisted it. But I remained undaunted, and the cats and dragons in my charge were uncowed.

I sat in my regular place on Salanraja's back as she dived into the frigid wind above the jagged peaks of the Crystal Mountains. My whiskers twitched, and the cold blasted at my fur. It found its way into the spaces between my furry coat and the leather harness with a second fur interior that wrapped around me from my neck to the rest of my body, stopping just short of my legs and my tail.

The black Cat Sidhe Ta'ra – my *companion* – had come up with the idea to provide all the cats, as well as our resident Sussex spaniel, with a second fur coat. The Abyssinian Esme and I had been mightily opposed to it until the winter at Bestian Academy had truly set in. Cats aren't meant to wear clothing, we'd told her. Not even collars if we could avoid it, particularly those horrible conical shaped things that humans put on us to stop us licking flea poison off our fur.

But then it got cold, and I mean really cold. The kind of weather that carries blizzards that will freeze you into an ice cube if you stay out in them for even a minute. The kind of cold that can crack your teeth and make your claws turn so brittle that they fall out – or at least that's how the old Ragamuffin back in my home neighbourhood had put it during his story of how he'd had to spend a winter on the high Fjords of Norway.

We'd had to fly to the closest village in the foothills of the Crystal Mountains so the local tanner could fit the harnesses onto all of us. It had been hard to get some of the cats to stay still, particularly the famous Cornish Rex who had complained that they were hiding away his beautiful white coat. But it was so warm in the tanner's workshop that no cat had dared run away. Multiple cats had moaned that they'd rather stay in there and catch rats for the tanner than return to the mountains. But once they'd had their armours fitted, they'd all said that they were too hot inside and had decided it was better to return to their dragons.

Though my harness had been itchy at first, I'd eventually appreciated the protection it offered against the elements. For the first time I understood why humans needed to wear clothing. It's a mystery that had always eluded the cats back in my neighbour-hood as to why they opted to shave off all their hair. There was one Sphynx cat in our ranks who had said that she didn't know how she would have survived without it. I can imagine how the harsh conditions had been especially brutal for her.

Now, as we flew through a cerulean sky, a low layer of fog rimmed the horizon. Salanraja and I took the lead, with a good two hundred dragon riders in tow. Other than Salanraja and the mighty Matharon who tailed us from far behind, the dragons of our convoy were all dwarf dragons, their size being perfect for the cats who rode them. The cats included my *companion* Ta'ra, a black cat who once had been a fairy, and the mousy yet vicious Rex himself, King of Cats in Cimlean City, a title which he apparently hadn't renounced since his decision to train as a dragon rider.

The white Abyssinian, Esme, who was once Bastet's daughter, also accompanied us, though she wasn't in training. Rather, from the back of her black dwarf dragon Gratis, she would provide the glamour spells to conjure images of our potential enemies.

I was the leader, and these cats I was to train had barely tasted actual combat. It was my job to show them all how it was done. After all, I had once vanquished the warlock Astravar and I'd fought many battles since. But then what do you expect of a Bengal, descendant of the great Asian leopard cat and the mighty George? During our very first days in our litter, my Bengal mother had told my brothers and sisters and me that our legacies were going to be legendary. Mine certainly had been so far.

"*There, Bengie,*" Salanraja – the ruby red dragon on which I rode and to whom I was bonded – said. "*Can you see it on the horizon?*"

"Ben," I said. "*Ben. Ben. Ben. Ben. Ben. When will you start using my proper name?*"

"*To be honest, I don't think I can change it in my head now. I think 'Bengie' has caught on too well. Anyway, you're meant to be focusing on the training. We have a reputation to uphold.*"

I squinted to try and make out what she was looking at behind the setting sun. Only just visible, there was something down there that was luminous. It was mist-like and humanoid in appearance, and in place of skin it had a substance that emitted a white spectral glow. Even more difficult to discern was the ghostly staff it held in its hand.

"*I see it,*" I said. "*A manipulator.*"

"*Are you ready?*" Salanraja asked.

"*Now...*"

As soon as I said it, Salanraja swooped down even further until she was almost crashing into the ground. She telegraphed her manoeuvre well and I leaned into her motion, turning to her rear. Salanraja grazed the ground with her claws, carving two trails into the snow. As she rose again, she lowered her tail for only a brief moment, but that was enough. Behind, I heard the swish of air as the dragons in convoy adjusted their formation.

There were no roars from the dragons and no yowls or shrieks from the cats. That was good; Esme and I'd initially had a problem getting the cats to do things. It wasn't that they were incapable of doing the assigned tasks, but rather of following orders. Particularly if they were hungry – they wouldn't even mount their dragons for flight training unless they first had a full meal in their stomachs.

I mean, I used to be the same, but I'd learned how humans and dragons often forgo comfort for the greater good. It's one of the few things I have learned from them. That, and the fact that most food tastes better cooked.

Salanraja's tail swished through the plume of frigid powder that she had disturbed, and I ran down it using my remarkable feline balance to avoid stumbling on the way down. I rolled over onto the ground, a sudden icy chill causing my muscles to constrict. But I wasn't going to let it kill my momentum.

I called upon my staff bearer – a giant white hand that guarded my staff for me – from the mysterious empty place it seemed to occupy in the space-time continuum. The staff it held had white crystals inset all along the length of it. Almost as if it were having a tantrum, the hand swooped down to slam my staff between my jaws and then disappeared into thin air. I clenched down on it, afraid to drop it.

Already power was surging through me, the white magic coursing through my veins and providing a warmth all of its own. The crystals on the staff glowed white, and I gathered the energy, focusing the very essence of my being into that single moment. My veins grew from warm to hot, and the air seemed to bristle with static. At the same time, the manipulator turned its wispy form towards me, and it pointed its staff forward.

But it was too slow; I already had a bead on it. I released the power stored up in my body and channelled it towards my target. A white beam surged out of my staff, and it hit the manipulator where its heart would be if it were actually human. It had no heart in fact, but a magically powered crystal at its core. There came a loud buzzing sound and a sudden whiff of ozone, then a bright flash of light. Once that faded, only a purple crystal remained, spinning in the snow.

Esme flew overhead on her dragon. The Abyssinian also had her staff in her mouth, its crystal glowing brightly. Light flashed, magical energy falling from the sky like light rain, and then the crystal that had belonged to the vanquished manipulator was gone. In its place, purple mist arose from the snow ahead of me, and the air took on the stench of rotten vegetable juice. Esme had wanted to make this simulation as real to the senses as she possibly could.

Soon enough two hundred manipulators had arisen from the ground, their wispy forms almost looking like a sea of fog approaching from the horizon.

"Now it's your students' turn," Salanraja said. *"Let's see how they do."*

"They'll do well," I answered.

"And how can you be so sure?"

"Because I trained them myself. I showed them all the tricks,

how to will power into your staff, and exactly when to release. Besides, they're cats. We learn faster than humans."

"That's exactly what you said during the last training session."

"I know. But this time it's going to be different. I can feel it in my bones."

"We shall see . . ."

But I was already starting to see, because deep inside I was purring with satisfaction as I watched two hundred dwarf dragons swoop down from the sky in flawlessly graceful manoeuvres. They'd received years of training before they'd even bonded with the cats, under the tuition of the mighty bronze dragon Matharon, who hovered in the distance watching them. The dragons grazed the ground just as Salanraja had, and the cats rolled off their tails in a perfectly coordinated pattern, landing just a couple of hundred yards from where I stood.

The dragons rose, followed by a sea of mist created by the disturbed snow. Out of this, two hundred cats emerged, covered in white powder. Rex and Ta'ra led the charge followed closely by Geni, the tailless Manx who had once been a daughter of Bastet just like Esme.

Meanwhile, the new manipulators moved faster than the original one had against me, already with their glowing staffs in their hands pointed at the army of cats. My hackles pulled at my back in anticipation as I watched. Would my dragon rider brethren take them down in time?

The scene filled with sparks and winks of light as the cats summoned their staff bearers. Two hundred large white hands appeared in the sky, holding the weapons that we had taught the cats to use. You'd think with all those staffs flying about that the staff bearers would crash into each other, but these strange hands always seemed to know what they were doing. Soon the cats had their staffs in their mouths, the crystals upon them brimming with white energy.

I saw Ta'ra right at the front with her golden staff in her mouth, its crystal glowing with fairy magic that highlighted the white diamond marking on her chest. The way that the fairy dust spiralled around her staff gave it an impression of substance. Ta'ra saw me looking and blinked twice slowly in appreciation of the attention.

My fur bristled as feelings of pride and anticipation washed over me. This was going to be the moment. The cats would defeat the manipulators and prove themselves in combat. Then we would have an army capable of defeating the five warlocks who had lost their souls to the dark force, *Cana Dei*.

Thus we would return order to the world, and we could all eventually retire to a palace that I'd decided we would build just like the Alhambra in the Fourth Dimension. I used to think that Ta'ra and I would just retire to a cottage, but I'd started to like being a leader among cats. In our new home, I would carry the respect they held for me to my grave.

The air crackled and smelled of pure power. A sound like thunder erupted from the sky, then two hundred cats unleashed their magic upon the manipulators. It sparked, and it popped, and it fizzled. Then, like a guttering candle, it went out.

There wasn't even smoke. The air was redolent with the stench of rotten vegetable juice – created by the dark magic that had defeated my students. This lingered for a moment until Esme cancelled the glamour.

I stared in disappointment at the vanquished clowder. I tried not to ignore their protests about how cold it was and how they just wanted to get back inside. They just wouldn't shut up about it.

Needless to say, I was completely unimpressed.

❧ 2 ❧

DISAPPOINTMENT

"Three months!" I cried at the army of mewling cats before me.

We were now in the Versta Caverns, and my dragon riding feline students were lined up in several rows in front of me. They didn't look happy about being lectured, but I didn't care. Their dragons were in another section of the cave, and Salanraja had told me that Matharon was congratulating them for a session of rather spectacular flying. Their reward was only having to perform twelve hours of flight training the next day as opposed to fourteen. On the contrary, my students deserved no reward at all.

Our chamber was big enough to provide space for us, and the crystals on the floor, walls, and ceiling provided a warmth of their own. They protruded out of stalactites and stalagmites on the ceiling and floor respectively, from which rimy droplets of water dripped into clay-filled puddles on the floor. The chamber smelled musty and earthy, mingled with the scent of cat.

Beneath their facets, the crystals displayed a vision of the exact same training session that we had been through, on repeat. Inside these caverns, the crystals were always displaying some kind of vision, be it one of the past or a possible thread of the future – some more likely than others. This time, the crystals had decided to help me out a bit by showing my students' repeated exercise in glorious colour vision so that they could see for themselves how spectacularly they'd failed.

We had reached the point where the magic in their staffs popped, sputtered, and then fizzled into oblivion. Meanwhile, light flooded out of the manipulators' staffs and hit almost every single cat magician on the chest, marking their defeat.

"Three months of training, and this is all you have to show for it?" I raised a paw and gestured to a large crystal next to Rex that displayed the debacle in full technicolour glory.

I waited for a reply, but all I received was unintelligible growls and moans. I turned to Ta'ra who stood on my left. She was the only cat who had managed to defeat her manipulator. But then she'd originally been a fairy, which meant that she'd known how to cast magic from birth.

"How are we ever going to defeat the warlocks if you can't even manage one simple spell? Why can't any of you just learn from this exemplary student here?" I gestured to Ta'ra.

I waited for a response, and for a while none came. Rex glanced around at the other cats in his proximity for a moment. Geni, the tabby-coated and tailless Manx sat next to him grooming her fur. Out of all the cats amongst them, I would have thought she'd have shown much more promise. After all, she was rumoured to be a prodigy who could speak to unicorns as well as being a daughter of Bastet just like Esme. But she just didn't seem to care. It wasn't as if the fate of the worlds hung in the balance or anything . . .

When none of Rex's comrades seemed to want to speak out, he decided to brave the gauntlet and stepped forward. The wiry Cornish Rex was largely white with a black patch over his eye that made him look rather mean. He glared at me with an expression of malintent. His breath stank of rotting fish.

"You know, Dragoncat, when I first met you in Cimlean City, I liked that version of you. You had oomph. You had gusto. And now, we all think you're being a little too bossy. We'd like you to tone down this military front you're setting up, because it really doesn't suit us cats, you know."

"He won't do anything of the sort," Esme said from my right. The alabaster coloured Abyssinian stepped close enough to Rex that her pink nose was within swiping distance. She stared at him with that penetrating blue-eyed gaze that I knew all too well. "Ben the Dragoncat is acting training commander here, and you are all to do exactly what he says."

"Or what, *companion*?" Rex asked.

I bristled at his use of the word. Even though I'd told Esme that I no longer wanted to be her *companion*, I had no idea why she'd want to choose the oversized rat, Rex. I mean I knew the Cimlean King of Cats had prestige and everything, but still he was half Esme's size.

A few cats let out soft mewls that would have equated in the human language to appreciative chuckles, but Esme was having none of this discordance. She outranked every single cat here, including myself.

There came a flash of light, then Esme's staff bearer appeared and thrust her staff between her jaws.

"Dare you challenge me?" Esme's words didn't come out of her mouth, but from the furiously pulsing crystal on her staff.

Whiskers, she was only going to make things worse. The cats

would later accuse her of using human means to try to resolve cat conflicts. I decided to intervene.

"That's enough!" I cried, in the loudest yowl I could muster. "No food until this evening for all of you, and Rex for your impudence you shall fast until breakfast tomorrow. And we shall also have some extra magical training sessions today, which means less sleep for all of you."

Again I received a chorus of growls and groans from the cats, but none seemed ready to argue back. None except Rex, that was, who sidestepped around Esme then approached to face me head on.

He hissed at me and the hackles rose on his back. I replied with an equally fierce hiss, and we started to circle each other.

Esme turned around to watch, her head cocked, and even Ta'ra backed away. The mewling and moaning of the other cats fell to a stunned silence. Every cat in this chamber knew not to interfere when two strong cats come face to face, although with Rex's size I'd never have imagined him to be particularly strong. Still, he was quick-pawed and by the time I'd had a chance to swipe at him he might already be on my back nibbling at my ear.

"You know – you're a hypocrite, Dragoncat." Rex said.

"And you haven't got an ounce of grace in you," I replied.

"And here you're trying to teach us how to use magic in three months, when we all know that you took almost a year to learn any magic yourself. If only you could stop bossing us around and make us feel good about things. You don't seem to know how to make others believe that they can win."

I was trying not to listen to him. Instead, I continued with my own line of assault: "How they anointed you as King of Cats in Cimlean City I have no idea."

"Are you listening to me, Dragoncat? You are an imposter."

"No," I said. "*You* are the imposter. They call you the King of

Cats, but out of everyone here you are the worst magic user of them all."

That was the insult that sent the final hackle up on Rex's back. He hissed and howled, and he leaped at me. He hit me with such astonishing force that he sent me tumbling to the floor.

I don't recall much of what happened next. There was a flurry of claws and scratches. My limbs and mouth moved as if powered by a will of their own and no doubt so did Rex's. I smelled sweat, and I heard panting, and then there came a coarse barking sound.

Because there's no creature better at breaking up a cat fight than a dog. The newest beast to have entered the fray was Max, the Sussex spaniel who once could walk the dimensions. I saw a flash of his shaggy liver-brown fur, and then he started to bark. Given I could speak the language of any living creature, I understood exactly what he said.

"Wargs!" he shouted. "Wargs! Wargs! You are all smelly, meowing, wargs!"

I smelled dust and caught a taste of salty water on my lips. Then the yowling flurry of paws and fur was knocked off me. I turned to see Rex rolling across the floor, pushed along by Max's charge.

Rex yowled, lifted himself, and scratched at Max's nose. But Max was quick enough to pull his head back and then he growled and snarled, showing his big teeth. At that, Rex yowled once more and then he backed off, scampering to hide behind the rows of cats who had been our interested spectators.

Max didn't waste any time announcing the reason for his arrival.

"Look!" he barked, tossing his head up towards the tip of the largest crystal in the room. "Look! The crystals are displaying a vision! A vision of evil magic-wielding wargs!"

And all of a sudden, the room took on the stench of rotten

vegetable juice to symbolise the most evil magic possible. Fortunately, we'd learned from our previous encounter with the warlocks that the crystals were on our side, and they hadn't been taken over by the dark force known as *Cana Dei*.

But still the prophecy they foretold didn't look good, because the warlocks had found a way to break the worlds.

3

THE BREAKING

Set against the swirling purple mists and the pervasive odour of rotten vegetable juice, the crystals displayed the horrors of the future for every cat to see. Every single crystal in the chamber showed the same vision, across what must have been thousands of facets. They also provided their own sound effects and smells.

It was like being in a room containing only televisions – just like the one my master and mistress used to own in South Wales – with the additional feature of someone sitting just beneath you out of sight and spraying different types of perfume at your nose.

We saw the Darklands from afar, and the warlocks' famous seven-sided tower that reached into the sky. The building didn't stop at the top of the tower, because above it hung a stone platform suspended in thin air. The view in the crystal zoomed in, and then pitched around to look down at the platform, which displayed seven spokes as if part of a cog wheel. Six of the spokes were closer to each other than the seventh, which lay opposite the central spoke of the other six.

The platform revolved slowly around a hole at the centre that looked down into the tower as if into a bottomless pit. Currently the platform was empty, but green lightning flashing in the sky portended evils yet to arrive.

Originally, the warlocks had built this structure for their meetings since there had been seven of them at that time. But I had since defeated Astravar, and the other warlocks had succumbed to the devices of *Cana Dei* and in doing so destroyed their leader, Lasinta. This meant there were only five of them left to activate whatever mysterious power this contraption held within its walls.

There came a shriek from the sky which echoed within the chamber's walls. The crystals added an extra whiff of bird to the existing cocktail of rotten vegetable juice, and a buzzard came into view. The animal landed and a plume of smoke arose. The first of the human warlocks emerged from this, Ritrad the young, bald, and muscular one.

His face looked different compared to how I had seen him last. Now it had a network of blue egg-shell like cracks across it and his eyes burned with amber fire.

Next onto the scene came a seagull, cawing loudly into the purple sky. It landed and transformed, revealing Cala. Once you might have described her as pretty, but now her skin had taken on that same pallid appearance with those hideous cracks across it.

Junas came next as a vulture, hissing, shrieking and cawing into the sky. He transformed to show his lanky form, his skin again looking as pallid as the others'.

After him followed Pladana as a hawk. She landed, and after the purple smoke subsided around her she revealed her human form, small and wiry again with pale skin making her look a bit like a female human version of Rex.

Finally Moonz came as a bald eagle, who shrieked aloud and then landed on his spoke as the purple mist rose up to greet him.

He was an old man, almost as old as Lasinta had been, and now the way that *Cana Dei* had transformed his skin made him look even older. Like the other warlocks he had that hideous network of blue cracks layered across his skin.

The five warlocks stood at the ends of five of the spokes of the stone platform, with two of them remaining empty. Above the central hole hovered a crystal larger than any I'd seen here in the Versta Caverns. It seemed larger in fact than the new Great Crystal that had now been replaced in Dragonsbond Academy, where I had first trained as a dragon rider. From there, the crystal governed the general running of events, intervening in the assemblies called by the three overseers of the academy, the Council of Three – or six if you counted their dragons as well.

In fact I'd only seen one crystal as large as that, and fear spiked in my chest when recognition dawned on me. I knew exactly what I was looking at. I turned to Ta'ra who was sitting next to me peering upwards.

"That's the Grand Crystal," I said.

She turned her head quizzically. "The what? No . . . it can't be."

"It is . . . When we were in the Tower of the Grand last, we saw Lasinta touch it and fly away."

In fact, the White Guard kept this crystal safe and secure in Cimlean City, in the Tower of the Grand. It belonged to the king and contained the most powerful magic known to any living creature – so if the warlocks managed to steal it, that would have grave consequences indeed.

"There's no way it could be there," Ta'ra said. "It's heavily guarded . . ."

"It is . . . I can't tell you how I recognise it over any other crystal, despite its sheer enormity. But I've seen it for real, and I just know . . . It can't be anything else."

Ta'ra said nothing, but I could sense her fear from the scent of her sweat seeping out of her pores under her feet. The other cats around us also shared in the stunned silence, as if every one of us knew that the crystals were about to tell us something important.

The crystals spoke in a soft lilting female voice that almost sounded Welsh. It came from every single inch of the chamber, making it seem as if the place was rigged for a concert. They didn't use the cat language, but they didn't have to, because every one of us present would hear the interpretation in our own minds. This was the way that the crystals spoke to us, in what I'd come to call 'the language of the crystals'.

"*The young, gifted warlock's daughter, Seramina, had the power to break the worlds with her staff all by herself,*" the crystals said inside our minds. "*She still does, though she dares not touch her power today. But she isn't the only one.*

"*The Warlocks' Tower was built for such a purpose. It takes seven warlocks and a crystal of great power to perform such a ritual. And yet you see only five . . . but look again, for your eyes do not deceive you. Behold the Sixth.*"

A shriek louder and pitched higher than that of any eagle came from the crystals in the chamber. It caused me to instinctively flatten my ears against my head, but I soon unfolded them again as I didn't want to miss anything. Out of the purple haze that plagued the Darklands a giant form with dark wings appeared. At first I thought it had to be a dragon. But as it flew closer, I saw that its wings were composed of long feathers that writhed in an irregular pattern, and it had the fierce head of a golden eagle. Even closer still, I saw the powerful lion's paws and I knew this was no normal bird.

"A griffin," I said, for my crystal had gifted me with the languages of all living creatures and with them an entire canon of mythology.

"But they're meant to be extinct in all the dimensions," Ta'ra said. "Since the wars of the Pharaoh Warlocks, no more have graced the skies."

The griffin landed on a spoke of the stone platform and a giant staff appeared in front of it with a huge crystal affixed to the top. I had always thought griffins to be noble beasts, and as soon as I registered that thought the shape of the bird twisted again. It was as if it were a master of glamours and didn't want to reveal its true form, until I saw it. Its face writhed into the ugly shape of a big cat, with a gaunt face and jaw so long it looked as if it might fall off.

I had to blink a few times to see it, but its massive, outstretched wings didn't seem to be made of feathers and bone. Rather, massive snakes formed its pinions, twisting to the beat of the wings. Other, smaller snakes writhed around within the space between these, forming a membrane that never quite seemed to stay still.

"What is it?" I asked.

"I don't know," Ta'ra said. "In all my travels, I've never seen such a thing."

"It has a staff," I said. "That beast, whatever it is, might have stolen it."

"Or it's a magic user itself," Ta'ra said. "Have you thought of that?"

"Impossible," I said.

In all honesty, it had taken me months of trying to get my mind around the concepts behind magic. I just didn't have the interest for it, unlike the more studious Initiates in Dragonsbond Academy such as Ange and Seramina. I'd been more concerned with things important for survival, like food and sleep.

"*Cana Dei* is capable of many things," Ta'ra said, and she

looked as if she might have wanted to add more, but the vision in the crystal recaptured her attention.

In it, the five warlocks who were in human form had their staffs drawn and were using them to channel energy into the crystal at the centre. The spell looked complex, but their faces displayed no sign of struggle. The muscles on their bodies didn't move at all, in fact, as if they had turned into weird magical dolls. But then I'd never seen a doll which had that horrific fire burning at the back of its eyes.

Suddenly, the Grand Crystal glowed bright red and a beam flared out of it, pointing directly at a pentagram of light that had suddenly appeared on the empty space of the seventh spoke of the wheel. A white light came out of that impact point, stretching upwards. This widened to display a portal, an empty space leading into a fiery land.

The stench of rotten vegetable juice provided by the crystal took on an extra odour of brimstone. I almost feared the heat coming off the magma on the other side of the portal. But even more, I recognised the great demon beast who stood there: *Cana Dei* had introduced me to her so many times in dreams, before Seramina had failed the dark force and it had decided to abandon our minds.

The demon goddess was a terror to observe, with the mouth of an alligator, the paws of a lion, and the hindquarters of a massive hippopotamus. It wouldn't matter if it were on a dark night or in broad daylight, if you ever came across this beast, you'd be straight up the nearest tree and prepared to stay up there for eternity.

Ammit, the devourer, the dealer of death. In my dreams, *Cana Dei* had once told me she would bring oblivion to the worlds. Once they were broken, this demon warlord would be the first out, leading a swarm of invulnerable demon creatures of every possible type behind her. No world would be safe.

She stepped out of the portal and let it close behind her. The view in the crystals spun upwards to give us an overhead bird's eye view from high above them. I couldn't see enough detail now to discover exactly what was happening down there – instead, the view allowed us to see enough of the dry and cracked land to get a sheer sense of scale.

Seen from this far up, the stone platform looked the size of button, though I could see it was spinning slowly around the tiny crystal at its centre. A stunning display of lights emanated from its facets, beams and rays and prismatic pulses that extended over the land. Out of it, something more sinister had started to emerge: a tentacled cloud of darkness that I recognised all too well. A third stench added itself to the cocktail, this time of yeast extract, the signature aroma of *Cana Dei*.

Then it happened – there came a great crashing sound, and the darkness reached out like an explosion, blocking all light for a moment. Red cracks developed in the earth, spreading out like the rivers that precede a flood.

Out of them the demons swarmed. They were too far away to make out any details, but I knew they were facsimiles of every single imaginable creature. Except that demon animals are made of rock and powered not by blood but magma and fire, making them virtually indestructible. The view spun out even higher, allowing us to see the verdant lands and the lakes and rivers and seas. The darkness spread further out, erasing any colour, drying up any water.

We saw flashes of so many scenes then, this time back on the ground again. A black mist washing over a colony of cats in Cimlean City, leaving only rubble and ash. A verdant grove with trees, and unicorns drinking from the water, turning their heads to watch the darkness approaching – realising what was going to happen too late. Fairies dancing around a toadstool in the Faerie Realm, then the darkness washing over them too, leaving nothing remaining, not even the toadstools. In a living room that I recognised as being in the Fourth Dimension, a couple sat with a calico cat between them watching television as they browsed their mobile phones. Neither cat nor human had a chance to react before the dark cloud washed out from the horizon, broke the windows, and swallowed them into nothingness.

The dust settled, and all I saw was demon horses, demon flamingos, demon zebras, and demon hyraxes, walking the barren lands. Across every single dimension we could now see, everything looked the same.

This was the end – oblivion. The ultimate destiny that we'd all fought so hard to prevent.

And yet . . .

The vision stopped spinning, showing a lifeless, barren land, with barely enough light to see through. The chamber we sat in had now gone almost completely dark and so my eyes had already begun to adjust to see the faint purple glows in the crystals that swirled amidst the waving tendrils of darkness.

"*This is the future that will come to pass,*" the crystals said. "*If you fail to step up to your responsibilities and continue to squabble amongst yourselves. The power you all wield must come from within. It will take courage, and it will take a rare ability to see through the darkness to wield it. But the crystals wouldn't have chosen you as dragon riders if you didn't have such an ability.*"

"But we haven't even had enough time to train," came a loud yet scratchy voice from the darkness, and it didn't take me long to recognise it as belonging to Rex. "The students in Dragonsbond Academy take two years to become full-fledged dragon riders. We've only had three months."

My whiskers twitched at the cheek of the self-styled King of Cats. If I could see where Rex was at that moment, I would have swiped him on the ear for speaking out of turn. There was no point complaining to the crystals; they didn't govern the future, but only predicted it.

To atone for his insolence, I decided that I should address the question that needed to be asked.

"What must we do?" I said out loud, cutting off more random complaints from Rex. "What is the best action to help the threads of the future weave in our favour?"

The crystals seemed pleased with my question as they let out a warm pulse of light to acknowledge it. The darkness in the crystal faded away to display a verdant land, rich with flowers and butterflies. The air took on a rich scent of pollen.

"*Travel to the Tower of the Grand,*" the crystals said. "*For the Sixth warlock, the griffin, has a plan to steal the Grand Crystal within the next few days. If the warlocks succeed in gaining it, then they will have all they need to begin their ritual. Perhaps you will find a way to stop them, or perhaps other threads of the future will begin to unfurl. Only time and destiny can tell what will happen in the end.*"

The cats standing before me, now illuminated by the warmer light coming from the crystals, let out an elated cry. It seemed that they were happy to finally be getting out of these freezing mountains. None of them would have to wear their horribly itchy leather armour anymore.

I really didn't think they were ready for it yet. Esme, Ta'ra, Max and I could help. Perhaps even Matharon could play a part in stopping the theft of the Grand Crystal.

But this ragtag, untrained clowder of cat magicians didn't stand a chance against that mighty griffin we'd just seen in the vision.

"Who exactly should go?" I asked, trying not to express my concerns out loud.

"*All of you must go – every cat and dog present at Bestian Academy, along with their dragons. For it is only along this path that you can determine a better future for yourselves.*"

On that note, the lights coming from the crystals went out, and their voices disappeared from our minds.

4

FAITH IN THE CRYSTALS

We didn't have to go far through the Versta Caverns for the scent of cat to change to that of dragon. Because of their fiery breath, they smelled of sulphur with a little bit of burning coal thrown into the mix. One of them, perhaps, wouldn't stink out a room. But Matharon had all the dragons currently in Bestian Academy gathered in a single chamber, if you could call it that.

Despite most of the dragons now here being dwarf dragons, it still took quite a lot of space to house them all. The chamber Esme, Ta'ra, Max and I entered was so large that you couldn't see the distant walls. Only on the nearest one could I see the ledges that jutted out from the edge, featuring openings to a network of tunnels leading to sub-chambers that housed Matharon's Guardians.

The Guardians were old, retired dragons whose human riders had long since passed away. These dragons had gone into seclusion, spending the rest of their lives in the caves of the Crystal Mountains to watch the crystals for any visions that might cause alarm. Anything important would be communicated by telepathy to the king's dragon, who would relay the issue to the king.

Of course, this meant that the king already knew about the threat to the Great Crystal, and no doubt was making plans regarding how to protect it right at this moment. But then the crystals hadn't revealed who this griffin warlock character was. It could be anyone, even Seramina, the budding warlock who had almost destroyed the worlds.

The silver-haired young teenager was currently under guard at a private residence in Cimlean City, and she'd told me when we'd last spoken that she didn't want to touch magic ever again. But then she'd lied to me in the past and we all knew that she was capable of powerful magic even despite her staff having been destroyed. For all I knew, *Cana Dei* might still be whispering inside her mind.

There were other possibilities too. Really, this mysterious warlock could be anybody. A shiver went down my spine when I considered it might even be King Garmin himself. I imagined in my mind's eye his handsome features suddenly sprouting feathers, and his body's aging muscles twisting and popping, much like mine did whenever I turned into a chimera.

He'd always seemed such a nice king, particularly when you compared him to Rex, the King of Cats. He was in fact the only denizen of this realm who had fed me a meal of smoked salmon, having acquired it from his envoys in the Fourth Dimension. That kindness had to mean something at least.

But I'd been betrayed enough in my lifetime to know that you couldn't trust anyone at face value. I used to think the Sussex spaniel Max, for example, was the most vile and cowardly of creatures. But he'd turned out to be the bravest and most loyal character I knew.

The cave floor shook underfoot as I approached Matharon at

the centre of the massive chamber. The vibrations didn't come from the earth itself, but from the footsteps of hundreds of dragons, pacing around on their allocated ledges that had just enough space to allow them to do so.

Salanraja, who stood with her head craned high to stare at the crystals on the ceiling overhead, turned to regard us as we strolled past. But she didn't say anything in my mind. It seemed she was just as shocked by what the crystals had revealed as I.

Back when we'd last battled the warlocks, their leader Lasinta had died. The others, who had thus become mindless thralls of *Cana Dei*, had then threatened that they would soon break the world. But we hadn't really taken them seriously. After Ta'ra and I had tricked *Cana Dei* at its own game, I guess we'd subconsciously believed that the dark force had lost its power.

But *Cana Dei* was also my reason for being in the Versta Caverns. I'd come to train an army of dragon riding and magic wielding cats, so we could fly over and mop up the after-effects of our previous conflict. I suspected that the White Guard and the King's Dragon Guard were secretly happy that they didn't have to do it themselves; it did, after all, seem quite a tedious task.

If my students were as receptive to magic as I had been, we probably would have flown over to battle the warlocks already. Instead, we'd been living the last few months at an impasse.

Matharon seemingly hadn't noticed us approaching. The great bronze dragon instead nodded his head repeatedly as he slowly moved it from one side to the other, as if he were counting and cataloguing the locations of each of his dwarf dragon students. The muscles in his wings twitched, and he looked towards the passageway that led outside. No doubt he was about to announce another session of flight training, under the false assumption that we had time for that.

"Matharon," Esme called out in a loud yowling voice. She

spoke in the human language, because it was the only one a dragon was capable of uttering out loud.

The mighty dragon turned his gaze downwards. His wings, which had just about begun to unfurl, folded back against his body. I heard a couple of groans from some of the other dragons, and it took me a moment to realise that they were actually reptilian sighs of relief.

"So there you are," Matharon said. "It appears we have quite an ordeal on our hands."

"The crystals have instructed us to take the cats to the Tower of the Grand," Esme said, taking up the gauntlet as always.

"Indeed they have," Matharon said. He lifted his foreleg to examine a long, sharp talon. Everything about this dragon was impressive, from the burnished shine on his scales to the extent of his roar.

"But they're not ready," I added. "Apart from Ta'ra, I've not seen one of them cast a decent spell."

"Why thank you," Ta'ra said, and she brushed her nose against my cheek.

"You're welcome," I replied not turning back to acknowledge her. "Anyway, as I was saying . . . if we end up facing the warlocks now, we're doomed."

"And yet their dragons are quite accomplished," Matharon pointed out. "I've been teaching in Bestian Academy now for hundreds of years, and not once have I had a failed student."

I felt the hackles rise on the back of my neck. But I wasn't going to get aggressive – to start a fight with a creature like Matharon would be as stupid as that cat in my original neighbourhood had been, when he'd once scratched a German shepherd on the nose.

"What's your point?" I asked.

"Just that perhaps you need to push your students a little

more. It's only a suggestion, mind, because I'm a professional and I don't like intruding on another professional's methods."

"It's okay," I said. "I guess I could always do with some advice."

"Good . . . Because I don't know what the cats say when you speak to them, but I'm guessing they're always complaining, aren't they? That's why I take my dragons through such gruelling routines. They need to understand that there is no room for failure."

As I thought back to my fight with Rex, I pondered for a moment how I might have avoided it. The thing about Matharon was that he was twice the size of most other dragons. But then come to think of it, I was also twice the size of Rex and that hadn't stopped him from pouncing on me.

Of course, Matharon was right – we needed to get the cats to understand they couldn't seek comfort all the time. But given I'd been guilty of the same habit myself until very recently, I didn't know how.

I turned to Esme. "Maybe you should be their commander," I suggested. "You wouldn't allow room for failure. No one would dare challenge you in the way Rex just challenged me."

Esme stared back at me with her piercing bright blue eyes. It wasn't hard to tell when she was disappointed: her little pink nose twitched and curled upwards slightly in that especially admonishing way and her tail started to thrash against the ground.

"Do you not remember the vision, Dragoncat?" she asked. "You are meant to be the commander. You and Salanraja must lead the dragon riding cats into battle. If you don't stand at their vanguard, they may never learn to defeat the enemy."

I couldn't forget the vision, to be honest. The crystals had first displayed a version of it when we'd returned to Dragonsbond Academy, just after we'd stopped Seramina from breaking the worlds. It was the whole reason we'd travelled here, because everyone in the First Dimension knows it's unwise to ignore visions from the crystals.

Since then, they'd chosen to display other versions of the vision at break of dawn every morning. I'd seen us turning entire battles against magical creatures in our favour, hundreds of cats on dragons with staffs in our mouths, spraying fire, ice, thunder, and vines over a purple sky. They showed us bringing down thousands of bone dragons, manipulators, and all types of magical golems. Once or twice, I'd even seen us facing the five warlocks themselves.

In every single one of those visions, the cats had been accomplished magicians. But given our recent training exercise, I just couldn't fathom them getting there. Ta'ra edged forward as if she wanted to step between me and Esme, and stick up for me. But I glared back at her to warn her off. I was after all the great Dragoncat, and I could stick up for myself.

"Look, I know exactly how things are going to go once we reach Cimlean City," I argued. "I've seen through enough of these visions in the crystals to see how it's all going to play out. Maybe I've picked up on some of the destiny magic from the crystals, because right now I have a strong sense of the future."

Matharon looked intrigued. He cocked his head. "Oh, don't stop there. Please continue . . . I do like a good tale."

I took a deep breath. "I bet you we'll get to the Tower of the Grand okay, which will no doubt be heavily guarded by White Mages. Given King Garmin already knows about the inevitable loss of the crystal from his dragon, he will probably have posted some of his Dragon Guard to keep watch from the sky.

"Despite this, we'll no doubt encounter an ambush. The warlocks will already have a plan of their own and they'll somehow steal the Grand Crystal, because the bad guys never fail this early in an adventure. Then they'll use some powerful magic to teleport it away, no doubt channelling the might of *Cana Dei*. Meanwhile something horrible will happen to us. Maybe we'll have to fight demons, or Captain Alliander will arrest us all and put us in some kind of cat prison. Worse, perhaps the warlocks will kill us all and then we won't be able to fight another day."

Esme's expression became a snarl, and she hissed out some very rude cat expletives which are impossible to translate into the human language.

"Are you doubting the forecasts of the crystals?" she asked in the human language.

Max decided to chime in. "Dragoncat so negative." Recent developments in his abilities meant that he now understood all languages just like me. But still, he refused to speak anything but dog. "Dragoncat is behaving like a warg!"

I ignored him. "Why should we trust the crystals?" I asked instead. "They almost got me to kill Seramina. None of you got to see that, other than Ta'ra."

"But you didn't, because the crystals had a plan that kept all of you safe in the end," Esme said. "Everything that they've revealed to us has eventually served the greater good."

"I know all the arguments. I just don't believe that the crystals always have our best interests in mind. I mean what do they truly want? Does no one actually consider they might have an agenda of their own that doesn't necessarily work in our favour?"

"They want harmony," Matharon said, his voice booming so loudly that it caused a stalactite to fall off the ceiling. "They want only what it is pure and noble. That's how it's always been."

"That's what you've all been telling me," I said, "and I'll do what the crystals say. But no matter how much faith you've always had in these shiny lumps of translucent rock, I just don't trust them anymore. Everyone's got an agenda of their own. And a cat's agenda involves a good meal and warm place to groom and sleep, which is in the mind of every single one of my students right now. If we act now, we don't stand a chance against the warlocks."

"Your opinion is noted and valued," Matharon said, though his sardonic undertone made it sound like he hadn't paid much heed to me at all. "Now I shall tell the dragons to get ready to fly to Cimlean City."

He turned his head away from us to so he could give the order that he'd planned to give all along. I turned towards the exit and made my way back to the cats' chamber. I'd decided things would go much more smoothly if I went back on my punishment and gave the cats permission to have one last meal.

After all, I could think of only one thing more unfavourable than going into battle with an army of untrained cats. An army of untrained and hungry cats would be ten times worse.

5

CITY LIGHTS

I approached Cimlean City on Salanraja's back, accompanied by our platoon of feline dragon riders. As we'd seen in the vision, Salanraja led the formation with the more senior dragons flying behind – namely Ta'ra's alabaster dragon Kada, Esme's ebony dragon Gratis, and Max's shiny jet-black dragon, Corralsa. The rest of the dragons followed in a long tail, ready to form a flank should we encounter any bone dragons or other enemies on the way.

Matharon had decided that he and his guardian dragons wouldn't accompany us. Someone needed to guard the Versta Caverns, he'd pointed out. One of the worst things we could do was leave the crystals unprotected for the Warlocks to pluck right out and convert to dark crystals. Particularly given we'd seen them with a mighty army in some of the visions. We needed to do whatever we could to stop them from building that army.

The city itself didn't quite glow like it used to. When I'd first seen it from afar, the city had looked magnificent to say the least. Although the architecture was the same; the tall minarets hung over the stone buildings and the walls looked high and sturdy enough to halt a platoon of charging rhinoceroses.

Before, the whole city used to be powered by crystals. Housed in tall towers, these had once provided the denizens with light and heat, their magic flowing through the walls as if through a network of veins and arteries. Last time I had visited, *Cana Dei* had used these crystals to find its way into the minds of the White Mages, and so King Garmin had ordered them turned off.

This meant that only one tower now glowed brighter than the rest, and this was the high Tower of the Grand that loomed over the city like a tree over a field of grass. It contained the Grand Crystal in the massive solar at the top, which needed to be large enough to house two large elephants, stacked one on top of the other.

This was warded by powerful White Magic, that mages and unicorns renewed daily so *Cana Dei* didn't have a chance of even touching it.

We approached the city under cover of a velvet indigo twilight. Instead of glowing bright white, the stone now had a regular earthy-red colour, making the construction look like a cascade of packed mud. We approached by air, but flew low enough that I could smell the dust coming off it. The tower crystals had provided more than heat and light it seemed – they had kept the city clean, too.

Even so, the lack of magic gave Cimlean City more of a chance to smell of itself. Even from several miles away, tantalising aromas of mutton and beef cooking on braziers in the marketplace wafted towards us as if carried by magical currents of their own.

"The dwarf dragons tell me that their riders are complaining of hunger again," Salanraja said to me.

I looked behind at the dragons, the edges of their scales lit by the torchlight coming from below. *"Those cats will never be happy."*

"I remember when you were like that," Salanraja said. *"Everything was about food, food, food, food, food. Salanraja, can you hunt some venison for me? Salanraja, can we steal some mutton from those village elders? Salanraja, why can't we go back to the Fourth Dimension and get some smoked salmon? You'll like it so much."*

"You do realise that this behaviour is perfectly normal for a cat?" I said. *"It's your expectations that you can turn us into loyal dragon riders that has forced us to change."*

"How many times . . . it's not our expectations, it's the crystals'. Everything we've done so far has been in their service."

"Which is to say that they control us," I argued back. *"We don't have wills of our own."*

"Oh don't start that again, Bengie. You've been so negative of late."

"So prove me wrong . . ." I swatted at a fly that had not only dared to come up to our level but had also buzzed right next to my ear. As usual with such encounters between cats and insects, I missed.

"Fine, if you insist, though I don't understand why I have to explain such things. How would you react if you could see the future?"

I considered the question. *"Do you mean to ask how would I react now? Or how would I have reacted in the past?"*

"Both . . . Is there any difference?"

The fly came in for another pass, and this time I watched it, ready to pounce, but again it flew out of reach. *"I guess there isn't . . ."*

"So? Stop chasing flies and focus on the question."

"I don't know . . . It depends how hungry I was."

"Fine, if you're going to be like that, I'll tell you how you'd react

– because I've seen enough of your mind to know you pretty well. You'd get all anxious about it, and you'd vacillate on the outcome for hours before finally deciding to do something about it. That's just how it is. The crystals show us what will happen if we don't change our course, and if the outcome is bad we adjust accordingly."

"Apart from the fact they select exactly what they want to show us," I pointed out, *"and they also seem to neglect certain details."*

"Because those details might cause us to act in unwanted ways. It's just as Matharon said: the crystals work to sustain harmony, not to create chaos."

"Do you really believe that?" I asked.

"Yes, I do. If it were any different, Cana Dei *would have destroyed us by now."*

I had no answer to that. It had been the crystals' idea to get me to make a deal with *Cana Dei* that had allowed us to trick the dark force and beat it at its own game. But if I'd made that deal knowing exactly what the crystals were up to, *Cana Dei* would have told Seramina their plans and we wouldn't have been able to stop her from destroying the worlds.

I continued to watch the night continue to fall, and the distant flickering of torchlight. If I hadn't been so acclimatised, I probably would have found it to be freezing up here. It was early winter after all. Instead, in comparison to flights over the Crystal Mountains, it felt like a sauna. I imagined that I might soon lose my armour, which had started to itch underneath.

Meanwhile, the cocktail of meats cooking in the markets continued to simmer in the air, making my tummy rumble violently.

All of a sudden, my gaze was drawn to something flickering in the city. In the shadows of a long street leading to the Tower of the Grand, untouched by torchlight, a bright pinpoint of light emerged. Then, on top of the other smells, I recognised a whiff of rotten vegetable juice.

"Whiskers," I said out loud.

"*What?*" Salanraja asked.

More pinpricks of light appeared. For a very brief moment, the city looked as if it were bespeckled with starlight. The smell of rotten vegetable juice got even stronger. Soon enough, vertical slits of light expanded outwards from the pinpricks. I felt a sense of time slowing down as my ears perked up. I heard the steady beating of dragon wings, the gently swishing wind, and then the braying of thousands of unicorns.

The slits expanded outwards, unfolding the fabric of space time itself. They formed long oval holes that opened up onto a purple landscape. Portals that led to another place. Through them, I could vaguely make out the wispy glowing forms of manipulators and the lumbering bodies of much larger golems.

Our enemies streamed out of what must have been hundreds of portals with utmost efficiency. Even from above, it wasn't difficult to trace the manoeuvres of the armies. They moved unlike any natural force, powered by a vast kind of intelligence.

It didn't take a genius to realise that what we were seeing was the work of *Cana Dei.*

6

INVASION

C imlean City, which had been silent and undisturbed up until a moment ago, was now shining with the wispy forms of what must have been thousands of magical manipulators. They streamed out of the portals like water from burst pipes. The air stank more putridly of rotten vegetable juice every second, the smell carried over thermal currents created by the heat of the fire golems below.

"*Whiskers, it's an invasion,*" I said. "*The warlocks have decided to attack.*"

"*What in the Seventh Dimension?*" Salanraja said. "*How did they build an army so quickly?*"

"*Seems like our 'noble' crystals neglected that crucial piece of information. Let me guess: not even the king and his army of White Mages knew about it. Or maybe the White Mages knew and neglected to tell anyone. Or maybe, even, the king knew and decided he'd keep the information to himself.*"

"*Will you just shut up?*"

"*Fine!*"

Salanraja growled. *"Just steady yourself Bengie. We're going in."*

"Where? To the city?"

"Of course the city. Where else do you think? The Willowed Woods?"

"But we can't! Our cats aren't trained well enough to fight an army of manipulators. If we go in now, Salanraja, we're doomed."

"Why do you think the crystals decided to summon us here? We can be of some help in the battle, I'm sure of it. Or if not, perhaps we can stop the Grand Crystal from being stolen away to the Darklands."

"But how?"

"Just hold on."

I shrieked aloud as Salanraja entered a dive, and dug my claws into her rough leathery hide to keep purchase. She roared out a command to the other dragons to follow and we were soon swooping down in a coordinated formation towards the city's south gate. There was a large landing area just behind that – a long field with the grass kept short enough for dragons to land on.

This was one of the few places we could get ourselves into the city quickly on dragonback. Human dragon riders were a fairly recent invention in the First Dimension, and so the city hadn't been built to accommodate them. In short, we'd have to reach the Tower of the Grand on foot.

Behind, the dwarf dragons formed a double-file line so as not to cause congestion. I'd run the cats through several training exercises on how to get onto the ground quickly should we ever need to. The dragons wouldn't even need to land if things went smoothly. After all, we'd probably need them airborne.

Salanraja gained speed as more portals opened beneath us. More manipulators swarmed out into the fields that skirted the city. Something within the ranks of our enemies had seen us coming. The manipulators beneath us extended their wispy arms and pointed their spectral staffs towards the ground in our direction. Out of them they cast beams of light that hit the thin layers of cloud high above. These shortened, and at the tips the shapes of hundreds of bone dragons formed. One of the hideous skeletal creatures opened its wings and flew right towards us.

It charged as its manipulator host continued to channel energy into it. While the wraith-like creatures of light below fed the bone dragons with magic, they remained invulnerable. The only way to defeat them was to first remove the crystal hearts from their manipulator hosts so our dragons could then toast their skeletal nemeses with dragonfire.

"*Gracious demons,*" Salanraja said. "*We're going to have to be quick.*"

"Wouldn't it be better to fight the manipulators outside of the city?" I asked. "You won't be able to defeat the bone dragons without our help."

"*That's exactly what* Cana Dei *wants us to do,*" Salanraja said. "*But the crystals didn't tell you to fight them. They told you to travel to the Tower of the Grand.*"

"Whiskers," I said. "Why can't they just make things simple?"

"*Fate is never simple.*"

I took a quick glance around to look for flying creatures, in particular a griffin. But there were no signs of any warlock either in human or winged form. I didn't doubt they were here somewhere though, probably hidden deep within the city and commanding it all, the voice of *Cana Dei* in their heads telling them exactly what to do.

"*Brace yourself, Bengie,*" Salanraja said. "*It's time to land.*"

She was just a few spine-spans from the ground now, and so I turned towards her tail. It swished once over the ground, giving me enough momentum to run down and leap off. Instead of stumbling, I turned my shoulder and entered a roll. Behind me,

Salanraja bounced off the ground and chased a bone dragon back into the sky.

I didn't even turn to watch her go. Instead, I sprinted to the side of the field, to allow Corralsa room to perform the same manoeuvre with Max. As they approached, Max barked out into the night, sounded incredibly excited about this battle.

"Wargs! Wargs!" he shouted. "We're going to fight the wargs!"

Max gracefully rolled off the tail of his great jet-black dragon Corralsa. He ran to the side, we looked at each other, then we summoned our staff bearers. One giant white hand holding my staff and a pair of gauntleted white hands double-handedly holding Max's staff materialised in the air, and they plunged our staffs into our mouths. They were both White Mage staffs now, with small crystals inset along the length of the wood.

Other cats continued to land, rolling off onto the ground just like Max and I had. No single cat did this badly. After all, we were much more agile than any humans, with spines designed for this kind of stuff. Only Esme and Ta'ra also summoned their staff bearers. Esme's staff looked just like Max's and mine, but Ta'ra's was different. Made of no substance but dancing motes of glistening fairy dust, hers was probably the only magical fairy staff in existence. She needed it because she wasn't a fairy anymore, but a regular cat.

"Ben, watch out!" Ta'ra called.

She rushed forward as if ready to protect me. I turned to see a manipulator pointing its staff at me, beginning to glow bright white. I had no time to react and Ta'ra wouldn't reach me in time. The air hummed with static and there came a sound like pealing thunder.

Then there was a flurry of claws and fur, as something rushed out from behind it. I felt a searing sensation underneath the fur of my face, and my eyelids sealed shut to protect my eyes. It was so intense that I felt as if I'd suddenly been wracked by a fever – one that would kill me within moments.

Then there was coolness, and I heard a vaguely familiar voice.

"Dragoncat," it said in the cat language.

I peeled my eyelids open to see a fluffy ginger Persian standing in front of me. It took me only a moment to recognise him: this was Rex's 'brother', the cat he'd left in charge of Cimlean City in his absence. He opened his round mouth and dropped a purple crystal – the only remains of the manipulator that had almost destroyed me – on the ground.

I took a moment to survey the scene. All around me I could see chaos – flashes of white and green and purple, magic spewing all over the city. Unicorns brayed, people screamed, and stone golems crashed their feet against the cobblestones, causing minia-ture earthquakes. The whole place smelled like a midden.

"Bruno," said a brash voice from behind me. Rex pushed past me and studied the larger cat with his beady eyes. "You've survived this."

"Stick to the rooftops as you say, bruv,'" Bruno replied. "Now what next?"

"We need to get to the Tower of the Grand," Rex said. "The rooftops you say?"

"Right on, guvnor . . ."

"Hang on minute," I said. "Who put you in charge?"

Rex gave me a sideways glance. "The crystals, of course. There's more to me than you think, Dragoncat. And given this is my realm, being the King of Cats in Cimlean City and all, you'd do best to follow."

I looked at Esme, who twitched her whiskers to say that she had no objection to this. Ta'ra also seemed ready to obey. Besides, I could see a good score of manipulators and fire golems rolling down the street to the north, sending up a trail of fire and light behind them.

Rex was right; we had no choice but to follow his lead. The tabby Manx, Geni, came up beside them, and the trio bounded up a ramp that led up to a low overhanging eave.

I was next to follow, and I didn't look back.

7

ROOFTOPS

There were no pigeons on the rooftops of Cimlean City. Nor were there any sparrows, or starlings, or jays. Birds have the fortunate ability to fly away at the first sign of battles or natural disasters – only the wind can stir them, and even then they are light enough to float on some of the strongest currents. Who knows where they'd all flown to once our enemies had started to stream out of the portals, but they had left the upper levels of the city free for us hundreds of cats and a single dog to have to ourselves.

I felt as if I were sprinting so fast that I'd end up tumbling head over tail. Acid burned at the back of my throat, and I could hear Salanraja saying something in my mind, but I couldn't put any meaning to her words.

Rex, Geni, and Bruno led the charge, and though it burned the muscles in my legs I put in my utmost not to fall too far behind them. It felt a bit like one of those weird races that I used to watch humans participate in on the television in the Fourth

Dimension – often, I'd wondered what the whiskers they were doing it for. I mean, it makes sense to run to catch prey or for food that a human had served out for you. But you can recuperate from short sprints relatively quickly, as long as you stay in shape. What had never made sense to me is why you would run for miles to stay ahead of another person so you could be the first to charge through some flimsy ribbon that couldn't even stop a fly.

I've said it many times, and I'll say it again: humans are weird creatures. Even after working with them for so long, I'd never really come to understand them. Yet on these rooftops on this particular day, I was behaving in the same bizarre fashion.

But then I didn't want Rex to show himself as the leader in this scenario; I didn't want him to show me up as a slowcoach. What would the other cats think of their mighty Dragoncat, descendant of the great Asian leopard cat, then? Particularly after our fight in the Versta Caverns.

Therefore I sprinted just as I'd raced the desert cheetah in the Sahara all those months ago. I sprinted like there was smoked salmon dangling from the tail of a fleeing ostrich, and I wasn't going to lose my prey. I sprinted like there was neither tomorrow nor today, only the wind at my face and the rhythm of my claws scratching the tiles.

And for an extended moment it looked like I'd overtake Rex. He might have been king of these rooftops, but he wasn't a Bengal – the mightiest breed of them all.

I heard Ta'ra scream from behind me, "Ben, slow down."

Slow down? No way! I wasn't going to let my *companion* steal Ben's thunder. Both Rex and I slid around a corner, and I'd just about reached his tail and was about to overtake—

Whiz-z-z-z. The stench of burning camphor. The heat of a thousand fires. The sudden blaze caused me to slow; I looked up to see a massive fireball spinning through the sky. Powered by a single crystal, fire golems were flaming projectiles that launched themselves upwards of their own accord, flew towards their target with extreme accuracy, and exploded upon impact. This one was coming right into the path I was skidding along, and I knew I wouldn't have the strength in my claws to stop myself in time.

"Warg!" Max barked in the dog language. "Watch out Dragoncat!"

"Ben!" Ta'ra shouted in the fairy tongue.

Whiskers, I had no time to summon my staff bearer. The heat was so intense that I'd fry within seconds. There came a flash of light, and a magical shield suddenly enwrapped me. I barrelled into this kinetic barrier that someone else had summoned. I felt only coolness where there should have been burning heat. I breathed shallowly, though the barrier magically provided me with plenty of air.

The flames subsided, and I squinted to make out the spell caster against the fading light. At first I thought it was Esme, with her slender form and elegant posture. But this she-cat didn't have a pink nose, nor did she have the long tapered ears of an Abyssinian. Instead, she had long tabby fur and no tail, though she was still a sight to behold with the staff in her mouth and the white crystal glowing brightly at the tip of it. A giant white hand hovered in the air next to her.

"Geni," I said. "You can use magic after all, I knew it! That was some fine shield-work."

She turned away and I caught the smell of stale breath from right beside me. I turned to see Rex staring at me through his beady eyes. The commotion had clearly caused him to stop his charge.

"Dragoncat," he said. "Are you trying to get yourself killed?"

"I was trying to reach the Tower of the Grand," I said. "That's where we're going, isn't it?"

"Not dead, it isn't. Watch what's ahead of you and keep your whiskers straight."

"And what makes you think you have any authority here to give me orders like that?"

"Because you're in my city," Rex said. "And though I might be small to you, I have some awfully big friends."

He turned to look at Bruno who gave him a nod. I felt my back begin to arch and part of me wanted to finish the fight that Max had broken up before. But Bruno was looking at me in an incredibly unpleasant way, and that Persian was one of the meanest looking cats I'd ever seen.

Suddenly, there came another whizzing sound from below, and soon enough a fire golem soared into the air. I ducked and watched it swoop overhead. It splashed out into flames over the next street below, setting fire to a wooden stall propped up against a brick wall. Fortunately no one was there to be hurt. But the warlocks hadn't brought the magical creatures into the city to kill; they wanted to create a distraction to keep the troops away from the Tower of the Grand.

"Will you two stop bickering?" Esme said, catching up with us. "We're on a mission here."

"Yes, ma'am," Rex said, and he twitched his nose – the cat equivalent of a salute. But he did so with such awkward timing that he was clearly making a mockery of her. Really, I don't know what Esme saw in this impudent rat who called himself a king.

I looked down to the street, to see four soldiers of the White Guard arriving at the flaming stall on unicorns. They worked quickly, drawing their staffs. Both the magical instruments and the unicorns' horns glowed. They cast upon the fire a fountain of white magic that looked a little like falling snow, though snow didn't quite glisten like this did. It also made short work of the flames.

"So much fun!" came Max's hoarse bark from behind us. "So much fun! Let's go and catch some wargs!"

One of the White Mages below looked up as if he'd heard something. But the magic must have been so bright down there that I doubted he'd seen any of us in the shadows. Next thing I knew, Max was charging past with his staff in his mouth. But it wasn't his legs that carried him; instead, he was feeding magic into a hovering board that he sat upon. It was just like those skateboards that younger teenaged humans liked to ride in the Fourth Dimension. Max's board didn't have any wheels and instead floated no more than an inch above the slate roof tiles. He halted himself by turning at ninety degrees then looked at us, his tongue lolling.

"Are you cats coming?" he barked. "Or do I fight the wargs alone?"

"Where did he learn to do that?" I asked to no one in particular, feeling ever so slightly jealous.

"Obviously there's a lot more to him than you realised," Rex said, and he went back to stand by Geni. Both of them turned their heads to look in the same direction as Max. Their heads lowered and I thought I saw a shadow of something pass overhead. I shuddered.

I followed the Sussex spaniel's gaze back towards where we'd been heading. The tall tower with the high solar sticking out at the top loomed over these rooftops, emanating a bright white light. It should have warming, comforting, but instead it illuminated the silhouettes of five shadowy figures flying towards it.

I recognised the shapes instantly: an eagle, a hawk, a vulture, a buzzard, and a seagull heading straight towards our exact destination. It seemed the warlocks had arrived . . .

"Whiskers," I said. "We have to go *now*."

I stormed ahead, not looking back to see who was following. Though Max took the lead on his newfound vehicle, I was once again the cat in front.

8

UNICORN SURPRISE

The great craggy fists of the stone golems beat against the magical barrier outside the gate of the Tower of the Grand. They made sounds like giant battering rams trying to break through a castle wall, but the shield held strong.

The wispy forms of the manipulators also streamed magic of their own at the barrier from their spectral staffs, trying to break the flow of White Magic that the mages and unicorns were casting to protect the ground on which they stood inside of the barrier. There were around a dozen White Mages sitting atop their unicorns, and they were all fully trained.

I watched the scene from the edge of a rooftop, with hundreds of cats – and one Sussex spaniel – lined up on either side of me. All across the city light and magic flashed, sending up the smell of rotten vegetable juice and ozone. Unicorns whinnied, and they charged around the city with White Mages on their backs, in an attempt to put out fires and still the chaos. The battle sounded like a cacophony of irregular drums, a sore sound for any feline. Dragons soared overhead, some of them chasing and others being chased by bone dragons. Shrieks filled the air.

I could feel Salanraja's vexation as three bone dragons chased her tail. But at the same time, she had one in her sights and a White Mage had conveniently brought down its host manipulator. I felt the heat leave my dragon's mouth in the form of a fireball, and in my mind's eye I saw the flames wash over the bone dragon that was her quarry. The thing disintegrated into ash and then I returned to my own mind.

"Good job, Salanraja," I said.

"Thank you . . . Must focus."

Once again, I surveyed the scene below, looking for a way down. If the warlocks were already in the Tower of the Grand, then we had to find a way inside so we could do exactly what we were destined to do to stop them. Yet even now, I still had no idea what that would be.

The first time I had visited Cimlean City, we had recruited Rex and his clowder to storm the Tower of the Grand. Captain Alliander of the White Guard, who had also been tutoring us at the School of the White at the time, had confiscated our staffs because she had decided we were getting too close to *Cana Dei*. But at the same time, we knew that we needed our staffs in order to stop it.

So we had fed our new recruits the best feast of mutton sausages they had ever tasted, and in return they had distracted the White Guards stationed at the Tower of the Grand. Our venture had eventually proved successful, though there had been plenty of twists and turns along the way.

Back then, the cats had taken advantage of a short leap from an awning onto the wall that surrounded the courtyard beneath the tower. Alas, the White Guard seemed to have learned from their mistakes and they had since removed the awning, so we couldn't leap onto the wall directly from the rooftops. Instead, there was a low network of terraces that led down to the marketplace in a series of steps.

The cats were expecting me to lead, and so I waited for a gap in the battle. Timing was everything. I took a deep breath, and then I leaped.

Ta'ra and Esme slinked immediately after me, and I heard the gentle footsteps of hundreds of cats following suit. We were on the White Mages' side now, and so we could pass through the gate without issue. Fortunately, our magical enemies were too engrossed in their task of trying to break into the Tower of the Grand. I recognised the lieutenant commanding the barricade as Lieutenant Larmend, whom I'd spent some time with in the Sahara Desert. Though we'd had some run-ins, he wasn't a bad man. He also had a sharp eye, and he'd spotted us as soon as we hit the ground.

He lowered his previously-raised palm, commanding the White Mages to turn off the barrier temporarily. This allowed plenty of time for we fleet-footed creatures to swarm in. The manipulators seemed confused by this and cast another barrage of energy, and the golems charged. From behind them, some fire golems launched themselves into the sky. But by the time their magic hit, the White Mages already had the barrier back up. Thus not a single cat, unicorn, or human was harmed.

We passed through the gate without further issue, and entered the familiar courtyard with its short and neatly kept grass planted all around and irregular paving stones tracing concentric circles over the ground. The White Mages in the courtyard had dismounted from their unicorns' backs, and were fully focused on casting from their staffs into the sky. Everything was glowing and the air was filled with magic.

The cloud of white magic suffused the air like a veil, and it smelled of waterfalls and fresh pine. It brought an extra warmth to it, and within it I felt like nothing could harm me. Part of me at that moment wanted just to curl up on the ground and go to sleep. It had, after all, been a long night.

I heard the sharp voice of Alliander – the captain of the White Guard – and her shoes clacked unnaturally against the paving stones on the path from the tower's entrance to the gate. She had fiery red hair that she kept at shoulder length, and her cheekbones were so well defined that they looked able to sharpen steel. She wore the regular cloak of the White Guard with extra yellow pauldrons on her shoulders to denote her rank.

She also carried an air of superiority about her. She wasn't quite as pompous as her stepbrother Arran had been, but still she had a habit of brushing off those who weren't of high station.

I rushed over to the White Mage Captain. Esme, Ta'ra, and Max moved in towards me, leaving the other cats who (other than perhaps the mysterious Geni) wouldn't understand any of the human language at the gate. Her unicorn, Tanni, noticed us approaching, and let out a whicker as he sidled closer to the White Mage Captain. But Alliander didn't seem to have noticed our approach.

"Very good, very good," Alliander said out loud, surveying her subordinates as she walked. "Keep the protection up, and the warlocks won't have a chance of entering this tower. We'll keep it hidden between the dimensions until the storm passes."

"Whatever you're doing, Captain Alliander, I don't think it's working," I said.

I'd never liked the famous Captain of the White Guard, though King Garmin seemed to hold her in fairly high esteem. She glanced around as if to see who had spoken, and then she turned her head downwards. Her eyes narrowed when she saw me, and

Esme who had come to sit right next to me. She and the cats of the Academy had never been on good terms.

"Oh . . ." she said. "It's you. I thought you were meant to be up in the mountains training an army of dragon riding cats like yourself." She turned to a male White Mage with a mullet whose staff had started to lose some of its glow. "Private Carcoon, keep the spell focused for demon's sake. We don't want to make a mess of this . . ."

She turned back to me, and I waited until I'd recaptured her attention. "The crystals sent us here," I said. "They told us that the Grand Crystal was in danger. We've come to protect it."

"Did they now?" Alliander put her hand to her chin and cocked her head. The hackles went up along my back. "So you brought all of the cats here?"

Her eyes scanned the courtyard, taking in every cat present. As they did, the expression on her face brightened. Call it a feline sixth sense, but I immediately sensed something was off. The air had taken on a sudden acrid and almost familiar tang, and I wasn't the only one who seemed to notice.

"What's happening?" Esme said, and she blinked a few times as if trying to focus.

She was trying to summon her staff bearer, and as soon as I realised it I tried to do the same. But I couldn't find it anywhere – it had become lost in that space between the worlds. Panic gripped my throat and I gasped for air.

Alliander clicked her fingers and then drew her staff from her back. She held it steady and her staff glowed bright white. It didn't look like a stick anymore, but like a glowing shaft whose only substance was light. Her eyes burned with yellow fire.

I felt that same kind of shimmer in the fabric of space-time that I'd encountered the first time Astravar had pulled me through the portal into this dimension. Time stopped around me, the unicorns and White Mages looking like dolls in a child's toy house.

"You know," she said, "the advantage of being a captain of such a large magical army is that I can determine which magic they should use. I concoct the formula, and they just do what I tell them to do. Right now, they think they are casting a spell to hide the Tower of the Grand from the warlocks, when indeed it is the very spell that shall transport the Grand Crystal where we need it to be. It's beautiful, don't you think?"

I wanted to say more, but a lump had caught in my throat. I kept clutching in my mind for my staff bearer, but it was nowhere to be found. I tried calling to Salanraja instead, but I found only emptiness. Alliander's features twisted, and in them I didn't see the once stern face of the White Mage commander. I saw a lion, but not a healthy one. Instead, it had crooked yellow teeth and long, pallid face.

"What is this?" Esme asked again. "Who are you?"

"Captain Alliander." She studied her fingernails as if they were claws.

"Then I asked the wrong question . . . *What* exactly are you?" Esme asked again, and her voice had become a growl. I think she might have even said it in the cat language.

A cloud developed at Alliander's feet, but it didn't take on the deep purple that dark magic usually did. It stank even worse than rotten vegetable juice, so strongly that it seemed to burn the walls of our lungs.

"I am a powerful magician," Alliander said, and raised her hands. "Like my stepbrother Arran was, and you too could have been if you had played your cards right. Just like Astravar, and Arran, and your Seramina . . . All this time I've been a prodigy amongst white magic users, yet I'm so much more than that. The reason I'm so powerful is that I've trained in all schools of magic.

And when *Cana Dei* presented itself to me, do you really think I'd be able to resist its pull?"

Her unicorn, Tanni, moved closer to her. Except it wasn't a unicorn at all, but an extension of her, because it soon formed part of the swirling cloud that had started to envelop the monster that Alliander had turned out to be. Where the unicorn's body had been, there was a coat of writhing snakes, which merged with Alliander's outstretched arms to create the pinions of outstretched wings. Now her face had fully formed, and I realised it looked more like a mountain lion than the actual true lion's that I'd imagined my ancestors to have descended from.

I found some strength in my throat to let out a growl of my own. For a moment, I imagined I could envision my staff bearer, and I called out to it. But Alliander's gaze snapped back to me, as if she had power over my thoughts. The image in my head fizzled away.

Alliander's gaze went distant and then roved over the rest of the cats standing near the gate, probably also frozen in time. I tried to turn my head towards Ta'ra to see if she was okay, but I couldn't even do that. There seemed like nothing worse than not knowing the fate of my *companion*. I couldn't even smell her. For all I knew, Alliander might have already killed her.

"Like the other warlocks, and all the demons of the Seventh Dimension, I serve the dark force *Cana Dei*. And you too have served it by bringing our apparent victors right into our hands. Or at least you've managed to unravel the thread where the runt of a pedigree Bengal they call Dragoncat leads them in battle and destroys us before we can complete our plans. Now, you – cats, unicorns, humans and dog – will all suffer the same fate."

Her gaze turned upon me. I wanted to tell her that I was no runt, how mighty I was, and who exactly I was descended from. But even my mouth was paralysed, owing to her powerful magic.

Alliander raised her staff and a stabbing pain rushed to my head; I couldn't even twist my jaw to object. The White Mage turned warlock raised her staff and it flashed both with bright light and a darkness that seemed to rip my soul right out of my body. Again I saw that cruel gaunt mountain lion's face, grinning as if it was enjoying every moment of this.

Then I saw blackness. First I was spinning, then I was falling, and then I felt only nothingness before me and it reached out its tendrils to embrace me.

9

BETWEEN WORLDS

It turned out I wasn't dead, even though I could see nothing but blackness. Or perhaps I *was* dead, and I was on the way to cat heaven, or perhaps I was travelling down into the darker underworlds where all the bad cats ended up. I really had no idea.

I could hear my own thoughts, and around me I thought I could hear the sounds of a thousand cats meowing. I could also hear unicorns braying, and humans mumbling, and a dog barking. Yet my head was thumping so hard that I couldn't comprehend any of what they were saying. I understood none of it.

But I could hear my own thoughts, and I felt stupid. I should have listened to my gut, and I shouldn't have heeded the crystals' call and led the other cats to their doom. I'd said it before to Salan-raja – those crystals weren't to be trusted. Whiskers, I'd been so stupid, so naïve, like everyone in the First Dimension. . . It was like the two Savannah cats of my home neighbourhood in South Wales always used to say – the only creature a cat should ever trust is themself.

"Bengie?" Salanraja's voice came unbidden in my head, and I'd

never been so happy to hear her call the nickname that I hated so much.

"*It's Ben . . .*" I said, despite that.

"*Whatever, you're alive . . . I felt you enter another dimension. You fell across worlds, and I almost felt our connection split. But it didn't. Which means . . . Wait, I see the portal. Hang on, this time I'm coming too . . .*"

"*It's too late.*" I said. "*I'm dead, Salanraja. We all are. Which means, if you're talking to me, you must be too.*"

"*What in the Seventh Dimension do you mean?*"

"*Alliander killed us.*"

"*Alliander?*"

"*Except she's not Alliander* – Cana Dei *has taken control of her mind, and now she's become something else entirely. I don't know what she is now, but she's probably another warlock.*"

"*I don't know what you're talking about. Just hang on.*"

"*But I'm dead.*"

"*No you're not. You look perfectly alive from where I can see you . . . But fading. I need to be quick.*"

I felt the weight of a thousand dragon scales, and I saw Salanraja dive towards a field of gaping darkness, surrounded by a halo of white light. I only needed to glimpse it to recognise it as the spot where the Tower of the Grand had been. Yet it wasn't there now.

I felt a coolness on my own skin to mirror that which had passed over Salanraja's own. Then there came a sensation of weightlessness as my dragon passed the thresholds between the worlds. There was nothing above her and nothing below. She too had entered the darkness.

Again I focused on my own body. Smells came to my nostrils, of nothing at first and then the faint and nasty stench of yeast extract. *Cana Dei*. I heard the other cats again, my dragon rider students, their confused voices now intelligible. They weren't the only cats here either. The street cats of Cimlean City had also been transported into this place. I'd never have thought I'd see Bruno look so scared, but he was quivering so hard that he looked as if he might shake away his fur.

There came a thud against the ground that caused more than one cat to yowl aloud. But it was only Salanraja, and I soon felt her warm breath stir the air above me. She hadn't found me by sight, she had found me by proxy. None of us could see in this place.

Not yet.

Max was barking out warnings about thousands of wargs that he could smell but couldn't see. White Mages were screaming orders to each other to use the White Magic that they couldn't quite grasp in this place. And I had no idea what the unicorns were saying because they only spoke by telepathy.

By this point, my hackles were pulling at the skin on my neck, because I knew exactly where we were: Alliander had sent us to the Ghost Realm. The realm of all pasts, presents, and futures of everyone who has lived, is living, or will have lived. That, of course, included *Cana Dei*, who had made this place its territory, posing a threat for anything from another living realm that accidently found its way in here. The same *Cana Dei* that many times had been destined to destroy us all.

My whiskers probed the currents in the air, and I could feel tendrils within the darkness reaching out, searching. *Cana Dei* was looming closer, and if it found us here it could wipe out our existences from the annals of time.

"Everyone shut up," I screamed out in the cat language. "Don't say a word. Alliander has sent us to the Ghost Realm, and even by our breath it might find us."

I repeated it in the human language so that the White Mages would understand. Then I did the same using the same whinnies, whickers, and neighs as the horse language. It turns out the unicorns spoke the same tongue as their mundane brethren, it's just that they'd never uttered a word of it through their mouths.

It actually worked. My voice must have been so loud and authoritative at that point that I really did feel like a commander, as well of course like the descendent of the great Asian leopard cat and the mighty George. But I should have thought a little about what I'd said before I'd said it, because as soon as they had a little time to think about it, the cats, unicorns, and humans started to murmur amongst themselves once again. I started to smell panic developing, then I heard Rex's whiny voice cutting through the throng.

"So what you're saying, Dragoncat," he said, "is that we can't breathe, so we're doomed whatever we do? Where are you? I can't see a thing in this place. And what on the whiskers on your cheeky-cheeks is the Ghost Realm?"

"Just tell everyone they're going to be okay," I said. "You're a king, stop the cats from panicking."

"But you just said it's not going to be okay. I'm not going to lie to my cats if it's going to be the last breath they take."

"Oh, will you just leave Ben alone?" Ta'ra voice came floating out of the darkness. She'd been following my voice, and I could now smell her right next to me. "All he's done is try to protect you, and you always want to repay him with claws and insults."

"What would you know? You're not even a cat, but a fairy. One whom this strange creature who calls himself a leader has human feelings for."

"I'm a cat now, and a much bigger and tougher one than you are," Ta'ra said, a hiss in her voice.

"Yeah well, I can't see a thing right now. Because if I could, I'd challenge you to prove it."

"Allow me to fix that," Ta'ra said.

"Ta'ra no!" I said.

But I was too late . . .

I heard a fizzle then a loud pop from right in the air to the side of me. Ta'ra's staff bearer winked into existence with a flash of light, and it thrust her golden glowing staff into her mouth. I could see the features on her face, the shadows on her already dark form, and her slender outlines traced in gold. The fairy magic coming from her staff also traced the forms of a good number of cats sitting around her, as well as Rex who was right in front of her.

They weren't the only ones to notice Ta'ra's sudden appearance. From all directions at once there came a voice, rumbling and sonorous. I'd heard it so many times in my dreams. The voice of *Cana Dei*.

"There you are," it said. "At first, I found it hard to believe that Alliander had delivered so much more than unicorns and White Mages for my next meal. Now it is time to feast. Oh how I've looked forward to this. The mighty Dragoncat, his *companions* and his whole army, delivered right to my front door."

Again there came that horrid stench of yeast extract. From the shadows between the light being cast out of Ta'ra's staff, tendrils of darkness closed in.

10

THE REALM OF CANA DEI

They came through the light slowly yet steadily, the tendrils probing their way like ten thousand snakes hunting prey over a barren desert floor. Ta'ra didn't extinguish the light of her staff, keeping it clutched in her jaws as she watched the encroaching darkness close in.

We cats huddled together, and other White Mages drew their staffs. Esme and Max did the same, and soon everyone except me who could do so was casting out White Magic in all directions at the great blob of darkness that surrounded us, in an attempt to keep it at bay. The unicorns also summoned energy into the void, their eyes closed as threads of magic drifted out from their glowing horns, forming a wispy and cloudy barrier that pushed away the darkness. Everything smelled like yeast extract that had been applied to extremely burnt toast. It wasn't pleasant, to say the least.

I considered also summoning my staff bearer and joining the fight, but at the same time I knew it was futile. Our magic would eventually run out or enough of us would eventually tire. And still, despite their best efforts, *Cana Dei* wove its way through the cracks in my allies' magic. There was virtually an infinite amount of the stuff. Our exertions felt like trying to evaporate all the water in an ocean.

I searched around for Salanraja, but it wasn't hard to find her with so much light flashing everywhere. As the magic blazed and *Cana Dei* burnt at its fringes, I clambered up onto my dragon and climbed to her head to gain a better vantage point.

"*Please don't tell me you want to fly back to the First Dimension,*" Salanraja said in my mind.

"*What, can you?*"

"*And leave all your comrades here?*"

"*I'm just asking . . .*"

"*Well, no. You need powerful magic to open another portal, which no one here is capable of casting.*"

"*You can't just fly up from where you came?*"

I actually wasn't thinking of abandoning everyone. But if the portal Alliander had thrust us through remained open, maybe we could bring all the dragons here and fly everyone out. If we were quick enough, it might just work. Admittedly, we might have to leave the unicorns behind, given how heavy they were. But then, who cared about unicorns?

"*I'm telling you there's no way out,*" Salanraja said. "*Alliander, or* Cana Dei *as you say, summoned a one-way portal.*"

"*So why did you fly through in the first place?*"

"*Because you're always going on these adventures without me. I was starting to feel a bit left out.*"

She said it as if she were trying to make a joke. I didn't reply; I really wasn't in the mood.

Salanraja lowered her head. "*Look, I just thought I might be able to help. I thought I might be able to protect you.*"

"*From* Cana Dei?"

Salanraja said nothing, and I could feel that she felt a little foolish. One of the unicorns in the centre of our formation reared as it let out a loud scream. I snapped my head around to see one of the female White Mage lieutenants whom I had come to know quite well, Carmista, flop down in exhaustion and fall from her mount. I could see the consternation on the other White Mages' faces as they battled with all the magic they had at their disposal. None of them had ever faced a force like this before.

Cana Dei's voice boomed from the darkness beyond our protective shield. "Creatures like you, I've never understood. You know that you cannot win this, and still you fight. Why don't you give up now? You know it's so much easier to submit . . ."

I heard the whinny of another unicorn, and the White Mage upon its back – this time male – fell forwards into the creature's mane. The unicorn also had seemed to have lost its energy. Its head fell forwards and its eyes closed, but it remained standing on its sharp little hooves.

Our numbers were clearly dwindling, but still we held our ground. At the extent of the magic flowing from our forces, a sheet of white fizzled against the growing darkness. At the boundary, thousands of black flares jumped into the light and then fell back again, like fish jumping momentarily out of water. My heart was pounding, and I could feel the same fear that I could smell in the sweat coming from below.

Cana Dei continued its demotivating drone, clearly knowing that words alone would be enough to weaken our resolve . . .

"All I want is the one you call Dragoncat, who is a traitor to my cause. Step forward, you proud descendent of the great Asian leopard cat and the mighty George, and I shall not kill the rest of you. Instead, you can serve for eternity as my thralls."

I started to consider the option. If I could save my comrades, perhaps they would have a chance to—

"Stop even thinking about it," Salanraja said. *"Gracious demons, it's good that I came along. Otherwise you would have fallen for it. I know you would have."*

"But if we could . . ."

"No. You'd give it an even greater advantage that way . . . Do not submit like it wants you to. You're stronger than this, Bengie."

"Ben," I said.

Salanraja's skin rumbled underfoot as she growled from deep within her belly. I could feel the heat coming up from my paws, and I knew by the strength of the fire burning within her that she would rather snap her jaws onto me than let me answer *Cana Dei*'s parley.

For the first time, I saw the dragon rider cats perform an act of courage that caused pride to surge in my chest. First Rex yowled out an unintelligible war cry, and the white hand that was his staff bearer popped out of existence. Moments later, a good two hundred other staff bearers winked into existence within our ranks. With a few exceptions, the cats' magic was just as bad as it had been when they'd fought against the manipulators in Esme's glamour. But still, the pops and fizzles and whizzes added a little extra gumption to the fray.

Meanwhile, Ta'ra was casting out streams of magical fairy dust at the darkness. Where it hit her target, the streams turned into what looked like clouds of chickens that clucked and squawked. Maybe they would have been given life if it weren't for the darkness' uninterruptable power, which swallowed them like a swarm of hungry foxes.

Max and Esme were also putting on a good show, sitting back-to-back and casting out bright streams of White Magic from the blazing staffs that they held in their mouths. Their magic was so powerful that it also almost seemed to take on life of its own, casting patterns through the darkness so geometrically precise that I'm sure at least one mathematician stirred in his or her grave.

Some of the darkness condensed at a point of the magical boundary, looking a bit like the pupil of an eye. It swivelled around until I could feel it looking straight at me. Its gaze burned in my head as if probing into the very depths of my soul.

"I can see you there, Dragoncat," it boomed. "Staying there and watching from your dragon, whilst your 'comrades' and 'companion' stand and fight. Such a wonderful commander you are. Tell you what, if you deliver yourself to me then I will spare their lives and I won't take them as my thralls. Instead, all I want is revenge against you for your trickery. And I guess I should take your Cat Sidhe too."

That was the last straw. I might have given myself away, but there was no way I was sacrificing Ta'ra. So, instead of answering I started to give myself a good groom. By that point I'd decided *Cana Dei* was going to destroy me then it would take down a cat with clean fur. After all, I had my pride.

"So it's like that, is it," *Cana Dei* said, and all of a sudden the ground shook, causing Salanraja's head to lurch to the side. "You have no respect for that which is greater than you. None of you mortals do, which is why you must die."

It had been holding back the full extent of its power it seemed, because the darkness suddenly washed once again over the ground, erasing any colour that our magic had previously revealed. I heard yowls, and growls, and whinnies, and screams, and I felt something pulling me down, sucking on my insides as if it could pull them out on its own accord. An agonising pain washed over me, and I thought I would black out—

Until . . .

"Oh no, you don't." A familiar voice floated through the darkness.

It was young, and it was powerful. Familiar but also so much stronger than the girl I'd known before.

"Seramina?" I asked.

She appeared out of the darkness right next to where Esme and Max still sat back-to-back, her silver hair flowing behind her. In her hand she held a White Mage's staff, the crystals along its length brimming with an intensity of energy more powerful than anything I'd ever seen before. She stood beneath her dragon Halli-nar, whose charcoal scales seemed to glimmer with a magic of their own.

Seramina plunged her staff into the ground and sent out a shockwave, and all of a sudden the tides of the battle turned in our favour.

THE NEW MAGICIAN

The silver-haired young woman plunged her staff into the ground, and from it emerged a pulse of magic that spread outwards in a growing dome. Once again strength returned to my muscles, and I felt purer and full of energy. I almost imagined I could summon the portal that Salanraja had told me we would need to get out of here. Seramina's magic pushed back the darkness much further than that of the White Mages, unicorns, Max, Ta'ra, and Esme had combined, creating a threshold which didn't seem to cost much focus for her to maintain.

Cana Dei's voice boomed out of the darkness, its attention now focused on Seramina.

"You!" it said. "I finished you . . . You are not destined to return. Your story is over. You failed yourself when you failed me."

"So you might think," Seramina retorted. Her voice had the same kind of booming fire to it, with a power that could only be achieved by potent magic. I could see now that she wasn't the innocent and somewhat sulky teenager whom I'd grown to know and love. She had clearly grown, the cheekbones on her face hardening and her posture strong and commanding.

At the back of her eyes burned a fire with an awesome intensity, but unlike before this didn't contain an eldritch intent. Rather, it had warmth and compassion to it. She had power, and yet she could clearly only use it for good. Truth be told, I couldn't have been more proud of her. In the possible thread of the future that we'd found her in, she'd become the woman that I'd always hoped she would turn out to be.

"I was a destiny mage before you tried to bring me under your thrall," she said to *Cana Dei*, "and you know perfectly well the most powerful magic in that school involves the ability to elude fate."

"You cannot possibly be powerful enough to defeat the only creature in all the dimensions that is as old as time itself."

"Not alone, I can't," Seramina said.

She gestured with her staff in a wide circle around her. Esme and Max had already moved away in order to give her room. The other cats and unicorns had now also pushed outwards, given her newfangled barrier that gave us much more room to spread out. She didn't need to cast any streams of magic at the barrier to keep it stable; it seemed to have developed a life of its own, and *Cana Dei* couldn't penetrate it no matter how much it howled and thumped at the walls.

Out of the shadows, four more dragons appeared in the space around Seramina. One of them was more familiar than the others, for she had ruby red scales and two rows of spikes that ran along the length of her back, looking a bit like an inverted elephant's rib cage poking out of her sides and then curling back in on themselves as they led upwards. The dragon was Salanraja, and on her head sat a mighty fine specimen of a Bengal, descendent of the great Asian leopard cat. It didn't take me long to realise that this was a future version of me.

I also noticed the dragons of my friends. There was the great jet-black shiny dragon, Corralsa, with Max on top. There was the charcoal-scaled dragon who belonged to Asinda, the fiery-haired and cornflower-eyed young adult whom I'd not seen for some time. Then there were the two dwarf dragons, the black-scaled Gratis with a future Esme on top. Everyone looked so much more powerful than I'd ever imagined them.

"*Oh look, it's me and you,*" Salanraja said. "*I don't think I've aged a winkle. Though, Bengie, you seem to be showing your years.*"

"*Shut up,*" I said. "*I look magnificent when I'm older. Great and powerful like the mighty George.*"

"*You mean to say that you've put on a bit of weight?*"

"*It's all muscle . . .*"

"*Sure it is.*"

But I wasn't watching myself anymore; my attention had instead been drawn to a shimmering and massive feline form that had suddenly drawn itself out of the darkness. I saw pink outlines and a network of golden rings around her neck, and then I knew that Bastet had decided to grace us with her presence. She was a goddess who took the form of a giant cat with long ears, and she also protected our souls that burned within lanterns in the Fifth Dimension.

When she sat up, she was even bigger than I remembered her. As she craned her head high, I could swear she was almost as tall as Corralsa, who was one of the biggest dragons I knew, short of white Olan and bronze Matharon. Bastet gazed out at the condensed area of darkness that looked like an eyeball, now staring right at her.

In response, *Cana Dei* pulsed with laughter. "I thought you were getting supernatural aid, young Seramina. And now, Bastet, you present yourself to me. So you've been aiding the opposition all these years."

Bastet's voice chimed back against the darkness. When she spoke, she sounded just like the voice of the crystals that I'd become so familiar with, with a lilting female Welsh accent.

"That is not all," she said. "Just before we defeated your servant, Arran, I anointed them as my Guardians of the White."

"And what use are titles against the most powerful force that ever lived?"

"This is what you've always failed to understand, despite the many years you have spent in existence. It is not military might that matters but strength of companionship. That is what shall conquer in the end."

"Companionship?" *Cana Dei* asked.

"Of course . . . What use are Guardians without allies and leadership? Now, my Guardians of the White, show the darkness your true power."

She turned to look down at future Seramina. In response, the silver-haired young woman thrust her staff into the ground, projecting another sphere of white outwards. This time, instead of pushing back the darkness, it created life all around us. Daisies and grass appeared at my comrades' feet, and I caught a sweet whiff of fresh pollen, pushing away that rotten stench of yeast extract. The spell seemed to distort space and time, creating a large area around Bastet with wildlife as verdant as that of the Faery Realm.

Then came the smells of dragon, horse and cat combined. My eyes widened to see hundreds of cats, and they were mounted on different creatures. There were the same dragon riders that I commanded, but much stronger looking. They had staffs in their mouths with different coloured crystals affixed to the top of them. They clutched them with such confidence that I could tell they had become accomplished dragon riders.

Would become, I mean . . . These were all future versions of themselves. My heart swelled with pride.

But it wasn't the dragons and their cats that surprised me the most. For amongst our ranks was another clowder of cats also with staffs in their mouths, this time with crystals glowing all along the length of them. They were the street cats of Cimlean City, hundreds of them, and they all rode unicorns.

"This . . ." *Cana Dei* said. "This cannot be . . ." It paused as if to think for a moment. "Yet it doesn't matter. You can throw all the magic against me in every dimension, but you remain mortal. Your power cannot exist without me. And thus I must be looking at a paradox. Because without me, this future cannot come to pass."

"I think fate might think differently," future Seramina said.

"I also think that this *Cana Dei* is cramping our style," Asinda said, her voice also echoing around the walls of our safe haven, clear for everyone to hear. "Why don't you send us somewhere a little more private, Seramina?"

"Gladly," Seramina said, and she thrust her staff into the ground for the third time.

"There is nowhere you can go in here," *Cana Dei* said. "Nothing in this realm extends beyond my reach."

Yet Seramina's magic prevailed, because there came a bright pulse of white light and then the echoes of *Cana Dei* faded into oblivion, as if carried upon a distant breeze.

12

GHOST SAUSAGES

The smell of mutton sausages permeated the air. They were cooking over an open fire, in the courtyard that Seramina had magically transported us to. Though I had never seen this exact palace before, I knew exactly where we were. I could see the Tower of the Grand looming over the courtyard's walls, the solar at the top of it shining with the cool light of the Grand Crystal.

I also could feel an intense heat coming from behind the walls in the same direction. Though the other crystals that powered the city weren't within sight, I knew instinctively that they were there, shining brightly and sending out a web of heat across the magical veins within the walls. The grass beneath my feet was short yet soft, well-watered enough not to dry out in the balmy sunlight that shone down from overhead.

Everything was pleasant; everything was perfect. I could think of no better place to be. But at the same time, I knew enough of the Ghost Realm to know that this wasn't real.

Everywhere around me, cats and unicorns and dog, denizens of both the First Dimension and the Ghost Realm, happily munched on mutton sausages on the floor. I didn't dare to eat, myself. I'd been to the Ghost Realm before, and so I knew that the food here wasn't real and had about as much chance of satisfying a cat's dietary requirements as tofu. The White Mages didn't seem to know any different; they sat on benches set out along the walls munching on their sausages from scrap-vellum plates. These barbecues, after all, were a tradition in the First Dimension, and they weren't going to break the habit now.

Instead of eating the false food, I sat between Asinda and Seramina, Ta'ra cuddled up right between me and the silver-haired young mage. Esme sat on Asinda's other side. Salanraja stood by the wall between us and the Tower of the Grand, peering over it as she kept watch for *Cana Dei*. The only creature that was missing was Bastet, although in all honesty there probably wasn't any room for her in here.

Seramina looked down at me, and my stomach rumbled as I saw how much she delighted in the juices that flooded through her mouth. She didn't bother to swallow before she spoke. "I'm sorry, Ben, this must be strange for you. But our memories of mutton sausages contain a shared fondness. It seemed like the best place to bring you all."

"So why did you have to choose this particular memory?" I asked. "I'm so hungry, and I can't even eat."

"Would you rather see me trying to break the world again?" she said, and gave a wry smile.

"No," I said, not rising to her sense of humour. "Anything but that."

I really didn't want to remember how *Cana Dei* and the crystals had almost convinced me to kill Seramina.

"I'm only trying to get a laugh out of you, Ben," Seramina said. "After all this time you've really become so serious."

She glanced over at the future version of me. I looked at him too. "Well, I guess I'm glad that you didn't fill this courtyard with smoked salmon. That would have been absolute torture for me." I had only eaten smoked salmon once since Astravar had yanked me away from my breakfast of it in the First Dimension, and it was my favourite food.

"I wouldn't have done to that to you," Seramina said with a chuckle. From the way that her cheeks filled with colour, I could see that she was now a much happier person.

"Anyway," I said, "I thought you were meant to be the serious one."

"So did I, but I guess people change with time."

"And so do cats," I said.

Seramina turned her gaze back down upon me. Then her eyes went distant.

"I guess that moment of me almost breaking the world would be a bad place to go to anyway," she said. "*Cana Dei* can hear the emotion of anguish above anything else. It would hear your discomfort, and then it would come to attack us in full force."

"So why didn't you send us somewhere into the Faery Realm?" I asked. "Somewhere we could all just chase butterflies and have a good time?"

"Because that's where *Cana Dei* will look first," Seramina said. "In the places where you're all enjoying yourselves. I mean isn't that the obvious place to hide from the darkness?"

I scanned the courtyard, feeling mightily jealous over the smell. "It looks like they're having a good time here."

"Yes, but you and I both know that this will be short lived. Once they realise that the food isn't real, they'll feel even more hungry and *Cana Dei* will hear their pain. I wish to send you all back to the First Dimension before that happens, but first, you must listen to what I have to say."

There came an unnaturally chilly breeze from the south wall, as if the Tower of the Grand and the other towers in Cimlean City had stopped providing their warmth for a moment. I caught a whiff of yeast extract upon it, confirming that Seramina was probably right – *Cana Dei* would soon find us, and if this really was its realm it would probably return with reinforcements.

Some of the cats looked up in alarm, and a look of disappointment crossed their faces. They were about to realise that the food had zero value in their stomachs, and as Seramina had said their discomfort would only act to enhance the efficiency of *Cana Dei's* search.

"Tell me," I said, as I pushed my head into Seramina's hand. We may have been in a hurry, but there was always some time for a good stroke.

Seramina's face fell, and for a moment I saw the shadow of the apathetic teenager upon it that I'd come to know so well. Still, when she spoke she sounded incredibly wise.

"For those who are young in their real lives, the Ghost Realm provides so many more forecasts of their futures than memories. The world they live in holds possibilities, and both they and their fate will discover them for better or worse along the way."

Esme had now lifted herself onto Asinda's lap and started to express interest. With the light coming from the fire, her pink nose seemed to glow as she spoke: "I guess what you're trying to tell us is that this vision we're in might never even become a memory."

Asinda looked down at her and stroked her, but she didn't smile. While Seramina had become cheerier, she'd become much less talkative. It was as if the years had worn down her resolve somewhat. She looked, in other words, as if she lived only to fight.

"Hopefully you'll find a better solution," Seramina continued, "that doesn't involve us fighting all the time. You will have an opportunity to seal a new fate for ourselves. But you must be brave and you must seize every chance that you get."

I lowered my head. A part of my brain told me it didn't like this at all; it sounded like a lot of hard work. But then another part of me had learned to rise above it. I was after all a hero, a vanquisher of warlocks, descendent of the great Asian leopard cat and the mighty George. I was destined to be stronger.

"What must I do?" I asked.

Seramina nodded. "I hoped that you'd matured enough to make that choice. Now . . . Bastet?"

She turned her head, and suddenly Bastet stood in place of the South Wall of Cimlean City. She had her ears pricked up so high that she looked even taller. A pink glowing outline traced the edges of her tufts of fur, making her readily visible against the darkness that twisted behind her. Within it, if I squinted my eyes, I could make out how *Cana Dei's* thousands of tendrils had started to writhe and twist like snakes seeking prey. Just by making herself known, Bastet had revealed our location. Soon we would have to flee.

Bastet's voice chimed in that soft lilting accent, and she didn't even need to move her lips. "Regather the Guardians of the White," she said. "And then come together with your feline comrades and the dragons to the Fifth Dimension, the Realm of Souls. I have already gathered some unbonded unicorns, who have used their own magic to find their way to me."

"And what will we do there?" I asked.

"There my children and I shall train you all to be who you need to be."

"Is that all?" came a voice from below me. I looked down to see Rex staring up at her, licking his lips. He looked as cocky as ever.

Bastet turned her head down towards him slowly. She didn't blink as her golden eyes looked at him. He held her gaze. Clearly, he seemed to think he could challenge a god.

"No," Bastet said, and she didn't even sound perturbed by the tiny cat's challenge. "For Cimlean City is now in turmoil, and you must get your friends out now. Lose any of them, and we have lost. Even I cannot withstand the force of *Cana Dei*."

"Here," Seramina said, and she drew her staff from her back. "You will need to give this to me when you rescue me. Seramina will fight again, and this time she won't succumb to the will of *Cana Dei*."

The staff she offered was the most brilliant thing I'd ever seen. It was made of warped wood, with whorls and patterns that communicated its age. I looked a little closer to see etchings of dragons and unicorns and other magical creatures.

It didn't have that hideous and smelly purple crystal at the top like Seramina's old one, but instead crystals all along the length of it. Except these weren't a normal white like our own staffs, but they had a certain iridescence to them, displaying all the colours of the rainbow. The colours seemed to shift as Seramina rolled the staff around in her hand.

"You're not expecting me to carry that are you?" I said. "Because I only have one mouth."

Seramina shook her head and looked at me as if I were stupid.

"Fine," I said, and I summoned my staff bearer. It displayed no effort as it lifted Seramina's staff out of her hands and held it alongside mine.

"Now come," Bastet said. "All of you. As long as you remain here in the Ghost Realm, you are in danger."

She blinked her golden eyes three times, and the vision vanished. One moment many of us were enjoying a feast of fake mutton sausages, the next moment everything had gone – food, fire, sun, city, and all. We were left in the cold, shivering darkness that creeped in towards us.

There was a general growl and groan from our throng, but

that soon dispersed when everyone realised they were once again in peril.

"Follow me," Bastet said. "And run!"

A shining blue path cut through the darkness ahead of her, and she bounded off along it with the grace of a mighty panther.

13

RUN FOR YOUR LIVES

Behind Bastet, who was a goddess and would thus always remain in front, the unicorns took the lead. I could see their horns bobbing up and down above the feline crowd, and I could hear their hoofbeats against the blue shining path that had the texture of packed gravel and that felt as cold as dry ice. Fortunately for them, the White Mages had had the sense to mount their steeds first. Their clumsy human legs wouldn't have had a chance of keeping up in the Seventh Dimension.

Max the Sussex spaniel would have also been challenged for speed, with only his short stubby legs to carry him, had he not instinctively learned to ride a magical flying surfboard. Now the vehicle seemed to have become an extension of him, and he ducked and dived with it just as I imagined I did while on Salanraja's back.

It was okay for him; he could whizz onwards without any effort except what he fed into his magical staff. *Cana Dei* could chase him across the realm like this and it wouldn't catch him. Mind you, Max once could walk between the dimensions without the use of the portals, and I secretly suspected he still harboured this ability. The thing about that enigmatic Sussex spaniel was he never told you what exactly he could do. He just went ahead and did random things, surprising us all. Dog ex machina and all that.

I was too tired to run ahead of the cats this time – I'd already burned out during my race over the rooftops back in Cimlean City. So I kept a steady pace near the middle with Ta'ra staying close by, although she looked as if she were dragging her feet.

As we ran the ground shook, and many times it felt as if it would cave in underneath us. Or as if the realm would forget about gravity, if such a force even existed here, and we'd get sucked upwards like cats drifting in space.

Salanraja drifted ahead of us, tracing the line of the magical road. She wouldn't have been able to run across it at speed either, but Bastet's magic had accommodated for that. A stream of magic came out from the centre of the road, leading upwards to Salanraja and providing a protective bubble that wrapped around her. So long as she followed the line of the road, she'd be safe.

I couldn't see where the magical blue pathway led ahead of us. What I could see occasionally was the way that it twisted and turned through the blackness. It glowed underfoot, and the glow faded at the edges. All of us fought to keep in the centre, and I worried that the weaker of my students might fall off if they ventured too far out.

Even if they had, I'd have no way of knowing until we reached our destination. If they fell into *Cana Dei*, it would suck out their yowls and screams before the sounds had a chance to escape them. Once lost in that darkness, there was no coming back.

"How much longer, Dragoncat?" Rex asked from beside me, his voice coming out in pants and huffs. "I don't know if I can make it. My legs, they're slipping, and this isn't like the rooftops, you know."

"I can't tell you," I replied. "Just focus on the destination. We need to get out of here."

"I'm not sure I can. I should just stop. Leave me here. I've lived a good life."

He ground to a halt, and my head told me that I should just carry on. But I couldn't abandon him here, and I jerked myself to a stop too. His brother Bruno charged ahead, not seeming to notice that he'd lost the feline King of Cimlean City. Cats streamed around me, and I heard Ta'ra calling my name.

"Just go, Dragoncat," Rex said. "You're right, you are powerful, and I'm just a little Cornish Rex. Leave me. It's my time."

"No," I said. "I'll carry you back if I have to."

I looked up to see Salanraja overhead. She turned back to look at me, and I felt alarm spike in her chest. She continued to glide forward, following the glide of the magical road. If she broke even slightly off course, the magic flowing out of the centre would no longer protect her. Otherwise it would have been a mighty fine idea for Rex just to jump on her back.

"Do what he says, Bengie. They need you in the First Dimension. They don't need him."

"No," I said. *"Nobody gets left behind. Not on my watch."*

"But you don't even like him."

"It doesn't matter. You wouldn't abandon your dragon friends, would you? Even the ones who were cruel to you earlier in life."

"That's different. You've not known him that long."

"Still, he is under my charge, and I must protect him."

I turned back to Rex. "Jump on my back. I'll carry you."

"You've got to be kidding," he said. "I can see how exhausted you are. I mean I'm only little, but you know you won't make it."

"Just do it. I'm strong enough."

"No you're not," he said. "Go!"

He hissed out the last word with the same bellicosity as he had before we'd fought in the Versta Caverns. I could see I wouldn't get him to move on his own volition, and so I pushed forward to pick him up in my mouth.

"Ben, stop," Ta'ra said, who had just pushed her way through the stampede. "I can carry you, Rex. What? I'm stronger than I look, you know."

I turned to her, admiring the way that her green eyes glowed in the dim light.

"On you?" Rex said. "A fairy?"

"On the only cat who's strong enough and willing enough to carry you out of here," she said. "Unless you want me to take back my offer." She spun around and lowered her thighs to give Rex the opportunity to jump on.

"Well?"

"Fine," Rex said, and he scrabbled forward and limped onto Ta'ra's back.

"You can claw, but just don't bite," Ta'ra said, and she bound forward with an impressive speed. I tried to chase after her, in order to make it to the other side to at least congratulate her for such a heroic deed. Though my legs burned, almost as if *Cana Dei* had found a way to seep into them and pull me down into its embrace, I somehow managed to keep up.

The road wound in twists and downward spirals, and all around me I could feel the evil pulling on my fur like static in a storm. For a long moment, I didn't think even Bastet could save us. The journey had proved to be so long, and none of us had any idea when it would end.

But the end did come, in the form of a shimmering portal. I couldn't see exactly what stood beyond it, only tall stone walls and a lot of plants scattered around everywhere. At the same time, I felt a horrible burning sensation underneath my fur. Something other than my body wanted to wear me down and keep me in here. It howled like banshees in my ears.

The unicorns passed over the threshold, as did Max on his speedy magical board. Ahead, I could see the crowd getting smaller, and by the time I reached the portal back to the First Dimension, I was alarmed to find myself virtually at the back.

Bastet sat floating on the darkness that limned the fading edge of the road. By the time I approached her everyone else had passed through the portal, even Ta'ra and Rex. Bastet looked down at me.

"Thank you," I said.

"For what?"

"For protecting us."

"That is my duty," Bastet replied. "As it is yours to protect them."

She turned her head towards the cats, unicorns, humans, and dragon who sat in the other room staring back at me. It was only when a few of them blinked that I noticed time was passing much slower on the other side than it was here. All of a sudden there came a cry from the darkness, a howling rage, and I felt a sudden gust of wind. *Cana Dei* had latched on, and I had maybe thirty seconds until it destroyed me if that.

"I should go," I said.

Bastet nodded her head and said nothing, and I didn't even look to see what was following me. I summoned all of the strength bestowed upon me by my ancestors, the great Asian leopard cats, and I leaped through the portal just as it winked shut.

I hit a wall of shimmering cold, and then I tumbled over a warm wooden floor into the scaly foot of a charcoal-coloured dragon.

14

THE MANSION

The scaly claw I'd tumbled into belonged to none other than Hallinar, Seramina's dragon, who had helped carry the teenager through the darkness these last few years. Fortunately, in this world, every dragon I knew was on the side of good, because I know in many fairy tales of the Fourth Dimension they are not.

The portal had taken us to an indoor botanical garden, with tall stained glass windows set into the stuccoed ceiling, showing depictions of White Mages and Dragon Guards on their unicorns and dragons respectively. They spanned outwards in a concentric circular arrangement, with a large chandelier swinging softly right at the centre.

The place smelled of nature and had an intense heat to it. I gathered scents of thyme, and sage, and rosemary, and lavender, and other herbs clearly meant either for cooking or medicine. Fountains in the shapes of dolphins and fishes spouted fresh-smelling water into broad-brimmed bowls. I suddenly realised how thirsty I was and went to join the other cats and unicorns lapping the water from the stone bowl.

Of course, I made sure not to get too close to a unicorn as I sauntered over. It would be a fitting and ironic end if my life were terminated by the magical shoe of a unicorn's hoof.

As I drank, I listened to the sounds outside. The battle for Cimlean City still raged: I could hear dragons roaring, and magic whizzing, and the shrieks and crashes of our enemies. The earth shook with each loud sound, and yet I felt safe in here.

My stomach full of water, I took a look around again and saw the two large dark mahogany doors, wide enough when open to let a dragon in. That must have been how Hallinar got in here, but there was also no way for him to get out. The doors were closed tight and sealed by some kind of glowing barrier. If our enemies were interested in this place, they would have to work hard to break the magic. But who would have done such a thing, and why?

I didn't have to touch the magic to understand how powerful it was. I couldn't break it, Ta'ra wouldn't be able to break it, whiskers, not even Esme had that kind of power. I knew only one person who was on our side and in this world who could—

Suddenly, I caught a whiff of a familiar perfume: snowdrops, the scent of Seramina. I followed the aroma towards a stone staircase, which led up towards an open door. I climbed the stairs and entered the room to find the largest bedroom I had ever seen.

It wasn't quite as large as the indoor garden, but still it could have housed every one of us who had travelled through the portal, including the dragons if they would only fit through the door.

A network of neatly arranged parquet stretched across the palatial floor in a herringbone pattern. To my left the wall curved towards an alcove, containing a huge and comfortable-looking four poster bed. The mattress looked so soft that I reckoned I could sleep there for hours. A tall oval mirror stood on a stand opposite the bed, surrounded by a bronze frame carved with many kinds of birds. There was another door just by the bed, and a window with wrought iron bars across it, and the same magical barrier as downstairs spanning the width and height of the window frame behind that.

A much younger version of Seramina than I'd met in the Ghost Realm sat on a bench at the base of the window, gazing out despondently as if she had nothing better to do in the world. She wore the same white chiffon dress that I'd seen her wearing when I'd first met her within the realm of my own dreams. Honestly, it was as if she'd hardly grown in the last couple of years or so. But then she'd always had a slight frame.

I went over to join her, nestling myself into her warmth. She turned her head down at me, her eyes registering only mild surprise. She looked like she didn't even have the energy for that.

"Ben," she said, her voice floating so lifelessly on the air that it wasn't easy to catch it despite my superior hearing. "How did you get in?"

"Through the door," I said, cocking my head towards it. "It was open."

"Okay then, so how did you get into the indoor garden?"

"Why? You don't seem particularly pleased to see me. I said I'd come and visit, didn't I? Well, the descendent of the great Asian leopard cat and the mighty George has finally graced you with his presence."

Seramina let out a deep sigh, making it sound as if she wished I hadn't come. "It took a while."

"I had important duties at Bestian Academy, commanding an army of dragon riding cats. I suppose no one told you about that, did they? All of the cats who once inhabited the cattery at Dragonsbond Academy are now under my charge."

Seramina lifted her head and stared off into the distance. It was perhaps the most apathetic I'd ever seen her – a complete contrast to the more enigmatic version of her I'd met in the Ghost Realm. I clearly had a lot of work to do in order to bring her back to her true potential.

"I'm not sure what pleases me nowadays," she said. "And the recent hours even less so. I don't know what you've been doing, but in the meantime Cimlean City has fallen and the battle is lost. It's only a matter of time until they come for me."

I followed her gaze towards the view outside. From the window I could see the sandy courtyard of the School of the White, which meant her window looked south. Beyond that, the farms lay empty of crops, over which a convoy of bone dragons strained to carry a massive crystal in a giant harness. Other bone dragons flew around them in circles, protecting their treasure.

Whiskers, they had done it. They'd stolen the Grand Crystal, which meant it was only a matter of time until the warlocks summoned Ammit onto the stone platform and then worked the ritual that would break the world. I had no idea how much Seramina knew about this, and I didn't think it was a good time to break the news of what had happened to Alliander.

"Did you see a griffin?" I asked.

"You mean Alliander?" Seramina said.

The sudden abruptness of her reply shocked me into hesitation. Seramina didn't turn her head to acknowledge my surprise.

"You know who she is?" I asked after a moment.

"I only worked it out when she came to visit. It takes one to know one who's been consumed by *Cana Dei*. Then when I saw her fly past, somehow I knew. I guess it's because of all my workings with destiny magic."

"Alliander was here?" I asked. "Actually in this building with you?"

I still couldn't believe what I was hearing. In truth, I hadn't quite accepted that the White Mage captain, who was meant to be everyone's protector, had herself succumbed to the will of *Cana Dei.*

Seramina's ears pricked up and I could see the goosebumps on her skin. "She'd been so nice to me. Finding me this place, sending the White Mages three times a day to bring me food. Bringing me wool and knitting needles and embroidery kits to pass the time. When she met me just at the border of the Wastelands to collect me, I thought she would throw me in prison and leave me there to rot for the rest of my days. But instead, she gave me this tower to live in for the rest of my life." She swept a hand around casually to indicate the expanse of the room. "She treated me like a princess . . . She made it seem like this warlock's daughter, this traitor to the kingdom, would never see pain again.

"But when I saw her today, I could tell we had already lost. I don't know how long *Cana Dei* had been in control of her. I could see the fires burning at the back of her eyes, ever so faintly and I'm sure most wouldn't have noticed. And when the darkness told me through her mouth that it would return with company, probably the other warlocks, I could see it didn't want to control me anymore. All it wanted was revenge."

I growled. "I think *Cana Dei* has been working with her a long time," I said. "Remember that time we learned it had found a way inside the mind of the White Mages, just before Arran almost killed Bastet? I'm guessing Alliander had always been its Plan B."

Seramina opened her mouth to say something but was instead interrupted by a flash of light coming from outside. A fire golem projectile hit the top of a wall and erupted into flames. More light flashed from below and several magical beams burned a path along the street. They guttered out, and then I caught sight of five unicorns charging down the street, White Mages riding on their backs.

They didn't look like they wanted to fight anymore; they weren't even carrying their staffs. Rather, the guards kept ducking down on their mounts, their legs clutched tightly around their unicorns' sides. Even though the magical barrier behind the window blocked off the heat that had followed the explosion, it didn't seem to block off the sour scent of scared horse mingled with rotten vegetable juice.

"They're fleeing," Seramina said. "Most of the dragons have already gone, and me and you and Hallinar are about all that's left here."

She turned her head as there came a meow from outside the door. It was Ta'ra who had come looking for me. Seramina looked at her and chortled mirthlessly.

"You still haven't told us how you got here," she said.

Ta'ra came over to sit by me, but she remained silent. Instinctively, she seemed to understand that it was I who needed to talk to Seramina. Still, the extra support was nice.

"It's not just me," I said. "We're all here."

"Who's we?" Seramina said, raising an eyebrow. It was the most animated expression she'd displayed during this brief visit.

"Everyone I told you about: the feline dragon rider army under my charge, plus there's Ta'ra here, of course, and Esme, and that heroic oaf of a Sussex spaniel, Max. Not to mention the entire colony of cats of Cimlean City together with their rat-faced king. You remember how we treated them to the finest barbecue of mutton sausages that they'd ever tasted."

"It certainly helped to keep away the smell of the midden outside." A smile flickered over Seramina's lips, but it didn't last for long. "Still, I don't understand how you got in here past the wards."

I told her the rest of the story, of how the crystals had told us to travel to Cimlean city just in time to see the battle start. How we had crossed the city at speed over the rooftops, and arrived at the Tower of the Grand to be inadvertently sent to the Ghost Realm by Alliander so she could help the warlocks retrieve the Grand Crystal. I kept my narrative brief, though, as Seramina had already suggested that Alliander would return with the other warlocks soon.

"We came back as soon as we could, and future you told us that you can become powerful again."

Seramina shrugged. "Well, we're trapped here by powerful wards, so there's no way out. I don't have my staff, and even if I did, I'm not sure I have the will to fight anymore. I'm not meant for this, Ben."

That was when it occurred to me – all this time talking, and I had completely forgotten what I came to do. I summoned my staff bearer, and without dropping my staff, I willed it to drop Seramina's staff at her feet.

She stared down at it for what seemed like a terribly long moment; she'd probably been glad to be rid of that thing. But it wasn't the same staff. It was purer, and much less capable of evil. The patterns of dragons and unicorns seemed to swirl within the woodwork as it lay there, almost as if they had taken on a life of their own.

Finally, Seramina leant down and she picked up her staff with both hands. She touched it delicately, as if unsure what to do with the thing. But as she did so, the staff glowed with an energy that brought life back into her expression.

"Fine," she said. "Let's work this thing."

She strolled over to the door next to the bed, and within seconds she was casting the magic to remove the ward. It was as if it had been stored within her all along. She hadn't forgotten anything; magic flowed out of her staff in streaks and the air took on a kind of freshness, like an orange that had just split open on a cold day.

Soon the magic was gone, and we were free once again to leave the building. There came a knock at the door.

15

PIZZA DELIVERY

The air held still. Seramina extinguished the glow of her staff, and for a while neither I, she, nor Ta'ra said anything. I could hear my own heart beating, and if I listened hard enough I could hear Seramina's pulsing even faster. Though she had extinguished any light from her staff, she still gripped its haft tightly, her knuckles almost as white as the crystals.

There came the knock at the door again. The air seemed to stir around in the massive room. It brought a cold draught from the stone staircase beneath us.

Seramina looked at down at me, then back at the door. "Yes?" she asked.

"Pissa delivery," came a male voice from the other end. It certainly didn't belong to the other warlocks.

My whiskers twitched in surprise.

"Not pissa," said another voice, which sounded an awful lot like another old friend of mine, Ange. "Peet-zer. Like Peter but with a 'z' in there. That's how they say it in the Fourth Dimension."

"Peet-zer . . ."

"Good," the voice that sounded like Ange said.

"You've still not said why they say it," Rine, or at least the voice that sounded like Rine, insisted.

"I don't know; it's just a formal greeting they use when they knock on people's doors," Ange said. "Or at least that's what Asinda told me. She told me that she had some training about this in the Dragon Guard, just in case they ever need to go to the Fourth Dimension and meet our envoys there."

The knock came for a third time. "Are you going to open the door or what?" Rine asked.

Seramina took a deep breath. I meowed at her softly without remembering she wouldn't understand the cat language. But what I should have told her in the human tongue was she had to make sure it wasn't the warlocks. Fortunately, Seramina was smart.

"How do you know it's you, Rine?" Seramina asked.

"What? Don't you recognise my voice?"

"It's just I'm expecting more unpleasant visitors," Seramina said. "Company that has the ability to cast a glamour and try to trick me. So tell me something that only you would know . . ."

Rine, or perhaps the warlock who was posing as Rine, paused. I gazed at the door, my legs ready to flee if it burst into splinters; I kept a thread on my staff bearer and remained ready to call it in case we would have to fight. I looked back at Ta'ra. I could see from her arched posture that she was thinking the same.

"Fine," Rine said after a moment. "You told me once that you can never grow your toenails, because you think they come in quite handy as toothpicks."

"Stop it, Rine. That's a really embarrassing thing to say in front of people." The third voice that had come from behind the door was high-pitched and whiny. It didn't take me long to recognise it as belonging to Bellari, Rine's betrothed. Or they might be married now for all I knew. Knowing Bellari, she probably wouldn't invite me, or any animals other than dragons for that matter, to the wedding.

Seramina glanced at me again, then shrugged and opened the door. Bellari strode in first, her golden blonde hair much longer than I'd ever seen it before. It almost seemed to stream behind her as she moved. She wore a red cloak with a hood, and if it weren't for the red-crystalled staff on her back she'd look just like the innocent girl pursued by wolves in the fairy tales. But Bellari wasn't innocent, believe me. At that point, and for most of my time knowing her, I'd considered her one of the most odious humans I knew. Red simply meant she was a fire mage, and quite a powerful one at that. She was also High Prefect at Dragonsbond Academy, giving her considerable influence within the school.

Rine followed her, or rather was pulled by the hand. The young man was the one in Dragonsbond Academy whom the girls swooned over. He had defined cheekbones and sleek, oiled hair. His hair also stank of whatever horrible chemical he'd put in it to stop it from moving. He wore a bright scarlet gambeson to match Bellari's cloak, and suede leather trousers. His staff had a blue crystal on it – an ice mage's crystal.

Ange came in last, her head bowed. She wore simple clothes, a brown tunic with forest green undergarments, threads of cloth poking out in places. Her choice of colours matched her ability as a leaf mage, which meant she could manipulate nature magic however she liked.

A desert cheetah padded into the room after her, one whom I'd almost forgotten. I had first encountered Palimali in the Sahara Desert of the Fourth Dimension, when Lasinta had banished us there, many moons ago. On our return we had left Ange in the desert by herself, or rather the portal had closed behind us before she'd had a chance to pass through. Palimali had protected her there and had continued to stay by her side ever since.

During that sojourn in the Sahara, I'd had spent some time with Captain Alliander, and though she'd been stern I'd never considered her to be evil. But then I knew *Cana Dei* well enough to accept that it could consume the mind of anyone. Whiskers, I'd almost surrendered to its will, and I was so glad it didn't speak into my head anymore.

Bellari took one look around the room, her eyes roving over the bed, then the mirror, then the massive window at the end. "I heard Captain Alliander had put you up in fine quarters," she said, "but she's not who you think she is, you know? Aleam's waiting outside casting a glamour to hide our dragons. We're here to rescue you, because your life is in danger."

"We already know that, *Bellari*," I said with a hiss in my voice.

Bellari looked startled. She looked down at me, then her eyes registered surprise. "Why, Ben? Hello, I didn't see you there. It's been so long, how have you been?"

It surprised me even more when she reached down with an extended finger as if she wanted me to sniff it. She didn't try to stroke me or anything. Rather her gestures were those of a human who had met a cat for the first time and wanted to approach it with caution.

I looked at her hand, blinking without moving. Ange stepped forward to stand next to her.

"Give her a chance, Ben," she said. "I explained to her that maybe she wasn't allergic to all animals. I remember you telling me that your breed was hypoallergenic, and so we thought Bellari might be able to try approaching you."

Rine nodded. "Bellari really is a better person than you think."

Bellari's cheeks went red and she looked up at her fiancé. "Aww, Rine," she said. "That's so sweet of you."

I said nothing and did nothing. I was still looking at Bellari's finger, wondering whether I should swipe at it with extended claws or just completely snub her. That was when I caught the scent of catnip coming from the back of her hand.

"You've changed your perfume," I said.

Bellari turned her gaze back towards me. "Do you like it? Ange lent me some. She said it might help me get on with other animals."

"It's not bad . . . What do you want, Bellari? Why are you being so nice?"

"I just want to be your friend. You, and all the cats, have done so much for us. It's been me that's been so selfish, and . . ." Bellari took a deep breath. "I'm sorry, Ben. I'm sorry for being so horrible to you all these years." She glanced up at Rine. "There, honey. I've said it. Are you proud of me?"

Rine displayed a toothy smile. "Always, buttercup," he said. "Always . . ."

I blinked at Bellari rapidly. I really didn't know what to do or say.

"Ben?" Ange asked. "Maybe you can start to trust Bellari. She's on our side after all. And she's had a tough life, you know."

An irrepressible growl came from the base of my stomach.

"Come on, Ben," Rine said with a chuckle. "It's not like she's a warg or anything."

Though the hackles were still up on my back, my body was sending me mixed signals. Indeed, right from the base of my throat, I was starting to purr. I sniffed her finger. Behind me I sensed Ta'ra move to the window, but I didn't pay her much heed. Palimali also suddenly lifted her head, and her long ears perked upwards. She rushed towards the window to stand next to Ta'ra.

Unlike them, I didn't want to get distracted. I stepped forward to sniff Bellari's finger. There was no trace of the strawberries and cream perfume that she used to wear. Instead, she smelled completely natural, the way someone would whom a cat could like. I also noticed that she wore less makeup than before, and her hair was less groomed. It seemed that now she was engaged to Rine she cared a little less about her appearance. She felt less threatened, I guess, that she would lose him to another girl like Ange.

So I did something that I never thought I'd do. I touched my nose to Bellari's finger, and then I brushed my cheek against the side of her hand. She grimaced, as if she hadn't expected me to do this. But then she reached forward carefully and patted the top of my head. It felt a little awkward, but still it felt rather good. Cats are meant to be stroked.

"Uh, Ben," Ta'ra said from her place at the window. "I think we need to get moving."

"Why?" I asked, and I rolled onto my back displaying my tummy, wondering if Bellari would dare try and tickle me there.

"Can't you smell it?" Ta'ra asked.

Whiskers, she was right – there was something there. I rolled back onto all fours, and I took a sniff of the air. It had taken on the sudden stench of rotten vegetable juice, stronger than anything standard magical creatures could create. The hackles went up again along my back.

"Warlocks," I said.

Seramina's, Rine's, Ange's, and Bellari's jaws all dropped at the same time.

"Yes, Dragoncat," Palimali said in the cheetah tongue. "It's all five of them. And they're coming right this way."

16

MORE VISITORS

"*S*alanraja, tell Olan to tell Aleam to get the dragons to the back *of the building. We need to escape now!*" I didn't waste a moment sending the message to my dragon. Rine had already told us that Aleam had brought their dragons to the front, which meant that the warlocks would encounter him first.

Aleam was our old mentor, and the eldest inhabitant of Dragonsbond Academy. He had been Seramina's guardian since she'd joined the institution, and he also had quite a history of his own. Though he posed as a rare yet powerful lightning mage, he'd actually almost become a warlock himself. He would have done so, in fact, had his dragon Olan not brought him back to the light.

But though he was powerful, he wouldn't be a match for five warlocks with superpowers granted to them by *Cana Dei*.

"*Hallinar has already done that,*" Salanraja replied. "*It looks like Seramina beat you to it.*"

Indeed she had, because the teenager had been the first of us to spring into action and was already strolling towards the staircase that led to the indoor garden downstairs. She stopped on the top stair and turned to us.

"Come on," she said, beckoning with her hand. "This is our only way out."

Ta'ra, Rine, Bellari, Ange and I traipsed after her, not turning back to look at the room we'd left behind. We were soon down in the botanical garden, the cats around us looking awfully confused. All of them had met Seramina, and back then she was a human to be feared. She had after all harboured the power to break the worlds, and I didn't doubt she could still do so.

But Seramina ignored their moans and groans, and she went right to the double doors that Salanraja and Hallinar stood beside. My ears honed onto the sounds of flapping wings passing overhead, then landing behind the large double doors. The magical barrier covered them, and as I studied it, I saw all kinds of strange runes and I had no idea what any of them meant. The crystals had given me the ability to speak the languages of all living creatures, but that didn't include the ability to read written languages. Abstract shapes surrounded all kinds of weird looking symbols, flashing one after the other.

Seramina stood before the barrier and studied it. One hand was on her hip, the other held her staff close by her side. The stench of rotten vegetable juice came from the bottom of the staircase, floating down from the top of the stairs. I turned my ears to hear the clicking of a lock and the creaking of a door. The warlocks didn't speak in hushed voices. If we hadn't arrived before them, Seramina would have been up by the window listening to them approach. Without her staff, there would have been nothing she could have done.

"We don't have much time," I said.

"I know," Seramina said through clenched teeth.

From where she stood next to me, Palimali growled. She

darted through the cats that stood between her and the staircase, knocking quite a few of them squealing off their feet. Palimali soon stood at the base of the stairs growling, waiting.

She looked as if she thought she could take on all five of the warlocks. Mind you, the desert cheetah was fast enough that she could catch one of the warlocks by surprise, but then the other four would destroy her with powerful magic while she recovered.

"That's the spirit, Palimali," Esme said, and she also darted over to where the desert cheetah stood.

"We fight wargs! We fight wargs!" Max barked, and he barrelled along the path that Palimali had cleared.

Ta'ra moved in front of me, then looked over her shoulder. "Come on, Ben," she said. "We're the only ones strong enough to buy Seramina time."

She rushed forward and I knew that I had no choice but to join them. Palimali stood in front of us, lowered on her haunches and ready to pounce. Meanwhile, we four animal mages – Max, Esme, Ta'ra and I – summoned our staff bearers. The giant hands winked into existence and placed our staffs in our mouths.

Power surged through my muscles, warm blood pumping through my veins and filling me with energy. My mouth felt warmth where the crystals along the length of the staff filled it with heat. All four of us were powered up and ready for a fight.

The warlocks emerged at the top of the stairs.

17

WARLOCKS AND CANA DEI

Smelly purple mist seeped down from where the warlocks stood at the top of the staircase. All five of them were there, their pale blue faces marred with that horrible cracked-eggshell pattern. Their eyes burned with amber fire. My heart pounded the blood through my veins, and I tasted acrid saliva on the back of my tongue.

The warlocks stood in a line on the landing with Moonz at the centre. The two female warlocks – Cala and Pladana – stood on his left. The two younger males – Junas and Ritrad – stood on his right.

Together, they were the most formidable force I'd ever encountered, worse than Astravar, and worse than the Warlock Prince Arran. Worse than even Seramina at her full power.

Because each of these warlocks had *Cana Dei* thrumming through his or her veins, and all five worked as one.

Palimali leaped first, sending up debris and dust behind her as she charged at the muscular giant, Ritrad. The cheetah moved faster than an eye could blink, but so did the warlock. Just as Pali-mali left the ground, Ritrad whipped his staff downwards, sending a shockwave of energy along the ground towards the cheetah. Pali-mali seemed to hit a wall and tumbled backwards. There she lay inert on the ground.

The first bolt of magic proper came from Esme's staff. It blazed with such energy that it felt like it would sear my fur even though it never touched me. But Moonz already had his staff in front of him, and he spun it in his hands like one of those Catherine wheel fireworks. A magical purple barrier formed in front of him which deflected Esme's spell right back at her. It seared into the ground, rending up the earth underneath her feet and sending her sprawling.

"Wargs! Smelly wargs!" Max growled, and he let out a powerful magic bolt of his own.

This jumped forward in rigid sparks, heading straight for the once beautiful red-haired warlock, Cala. But she seemed untouched by his magic. Instead, she thrust her staff forward, and a crash of thunder came from just above Max. Lightning sparked down out of a sudden plume of smoke and hit him right on the nose. He yelped and dropped his staff to the floor.

Ta'ra then sent out a glowing spray of fairy magic that focused when it reached its apex into a spiral of golden energy heading straight for Pladana's chest. The wiry warlock let out a deep sigh and time seemed to slow around us. She performed a quick figure of eight with her staff, the two loops of this collapsing into two rings that flashed as soon as Ta'ra's spell hit them. Out of the colli-sion came a deep purple cloud, and out of this swarmed what must have been a hundred wasps buzzing straight towards Ta'ra. As the insects closed in on her, I feared the worst.

That left only me to act in our defence, and I had an idea. Clearly the warlocks were expecting a magical attack from my staff. Instead, I decided to try a different tactic. I willed my staff bearer back into existence behind Junas, ready to slap the back of his knees and then sweep him off his feet.

But before it could even wink out of the gap between the worlds, I felt something pressing at the sides of my head. Junas' face contorted into wicked slyness, and he twisted his staff to the side. It was as if someone had suddenly greased the floor beneath me. I couldn't find purchase on the ground and I slid and scrabbled, until I eventually face-planted on the flagstones.

There came an eerie, evil cackle from the five warlocks, and I say eerie because all five of them laughed together, their lungs heaving in unison. Then their lips parted, and they also spoke as one in a spooky and sonorous voice. The voice of *Cana Dei*.

"You thought you could run from me in the Ghost Realm," they said. "And yet here you are challenging me again. Now it is time to meet your demise – such a shame you won't be around to experience the breaking of the worlds."

They lifted their staffs together, looking like dancers putting on a choreographed show. The staffs glowed bright purple and the stench of dark magic became even stronger.

I willed myself to do something. Perhaps if I could turn into a chimera then I'd have strength in my rear goat hooves to charge them. If I could take just one of them down, perhaps I could break their spell.

But my head throbbed with pain, and I couldn't even focus enough to communicate with Salanraja. I turned my head to one side, only to see Ta'ra writhing on her back, her legs kicking out like those of an overturned insect. I turned my head to the other side, hoping at least Esme or Max had found some fight inside of them. But I couldn't move it far enough to see them, though I could hear Max whining from somewhere behind me.

I saw the warlocks bring their staffs downwards, the crystals at the top of them flaring bright lilac, and I closed my eyes in order to not see the end before it hit me.

"Oh no, you don't," Seramina said.

I dared to pry open one eye to see her appear in a puff of white smoke in front of us. She already had her staff clutched in both hands, and her silver hair whipped behind her as if blown by a gale. A wind picked up with the arrival of Seramina's magic, as if she were summoning all the air from outside and pulling it inside with her.

The magic thrust out of the warlocks' staffs, condensing into one wide and bright beam that looked like it would sear the fur from our skin. At the same time a protective magical shell expanded out from the centre of Seramina's staff, quickly growing large enough to protect us from the beam. Fire flared where beam met shell, letting out a scent like burning charcoal.

I'd been wrong about Seramina; now she did seem powerful enough to challenge all five of the warlocks by herself. There was something about that staff. She seemed to mould into using it, as if by simply wielding it she'd become the powerful magician she'd always been destined to be.

"You!" *Cana Dei* said. "You have your staff . . ."

I'd never thought it would be possible for an all-consuming and all-powerful immortal force like *Cana Dei* to sound surprised, but at that moment it did.

"Brought to me by my friends here," Seramina said. "A gift from my future self in the Ghost Realm, I believe."

She glanced over her shoulder at us, and at the same time she gave her staff a slight twist. The shell had now become a sizzling dome that shimmered overhead, and from its surface five threads of White Magic poured down onto my head and onto each of my fallen allies. I felt a sudden rush of relief, and energy returned to my muscles. My staff was still in my mouth, and so I clamped down on it with my jaws, feeling a new surge of power.

Around me, my comrades lifted themselves to their feet, and together we stood with renewed strength. The warlocks, or rather the *Cana Dei* that had consumed them, seemed to know it as well. Purple smoke had started to rise at their feet, and it quickly enveloped their forms so we could no longer see them. Behind the cloud, they turned their beam towards the window.

"You may be stronger than us now," *Cana Dei* said through their mouths in that spooky unison, "but against us, your former White Guard captain, and the demon lord Ammit you stand no chance."

There came five flashes of light, and five birds of prey – a bald eagle, a hawk, a vulture, a buzzard, and a seagull – emerged. The smoke dissipated to show them flying towards the window, and the ward that had been keeping Seramina in was thus erased. Off they flew into the predawn light.

It was only at that moment that I dared turn to see if the cats, White Mages and unicorns had already escaped out of the double doors that were also no longer warded. These led to a wide plaza, and across this expanse I could see silhouettes of my dragon rider students and Rex's clowder sailing over the distant rooftops. Dragons converged in the sky towards them, ready to pick them up and carry them outside of the walls.

No enemies were to be seen in the square, only black smoke and the embers of burned down stalls. Distantly, I could hear the crackling of fires burning. In front of all this, Aleam sat in the saddle on the back of his great white dragon, Olan. Rine, Ange and Bellari had also mounted their dragons – the emerald dragon Ishtkar, the sapphire Quarl, and the citrine dragon Pinacole respectively. In front of them, right where we had left them, stood

Salanraja and Hallinar. In between, Ta'ra's white dwarf dragon Kada and Esme's black dwarf dragon Gratis swept down from the sky, ready to land.

18

IT'S NOT OVER

T he sun began to rise into a clear and pale sky, casting a soft glow over Cimlean City that made it look as if it hadn't been attacked at all. From my position flying on Salanraja's back, watching the city beyond her tail, I could see no sign of the enemy that had attacked it. The golems, the manipulators, and the bone dragons had all vanished to other places. I had no idea how they had left. Maybe the warlocks and Alliander had sent them back through portals to the Darklands, or maybe they were marching towards the Warlocks' Tower overland, annihilating anything that stood in their way.

We flew south towards our agreed-upon meeting point, now comprising an army of dragon riding cats with a few humans from Dragonsbond Academy, not to mention Seramina who I guessed had technically been expelled. We had also now picked up Rex's original clowder from Cimlean City, and so most of the cats were riding in twos on dragonback. It must have been quite a marvel for the street cats to experience flight for the first time. I remembered how it had been for me the first time I'd ridden on Salanraja, although it seemed like the dwarf dragons were going much easier on the new riders than Salanraja had with me.

Beneath us bare meadows rolled by, devoid of colour and ready to be ploughed for the following season. A chill wind had picked up from the mountains, coming down off the highest peaks. Something had happened in that fight with the warlocks that had torn cracks in my leather harness. Now I could feel the wind seeping into the spaces there, causing me to shiver so much that my incisors chattered against each other.

There was no sign of smoke now from the city, and distantly I could see the White Mages on their unicorns surging through the streets and tidying everything up. Life would go on and they'd gain a new White Mage Captain, though I had no idea who that might be.

But then, if *Cana Dei* executed its plan, there would no longer be any life in any of the dimensions. Though we had brought Seramina her staff, our victory over the warlocks felt hollow. After all, they had escaped, and now *Cana Dei* had the Grand Crystal. Now they would be flying back to their base in the Darklands, ready to perform the ritual that would destroy us all.

In the Ghost Realm, Bastet had already told us we couldn't beat the warlocks without the help of my feline dragon riding companions at full power. We also needed to reunite with the fourth member of the Guardians of the White, namely Asinda. But we didn't even know if she as a newly recruited member of the Dragon Guard had made it out of Cimlean City.

Memories of the visions the crystals had shown us back in the Versta Caverns flashed through my mind. The way that they summoned power into the floating stone platform, and all the different ways in which *Cana Dei* then spread across the worlds. A shudder went down my spine as I thought of having to return to Cimlean City. What if Asinda hadn't made it?

"*You're doing it again, Bengie,*" Salanraja said.

"*Doing what?*" I asked.

"*You're getting anxious. I can not only sense your emotions, but I can feel the way that your claws are digging into my hide.*"

I looked down at my paws, and at the tough leathery scales beneath them. "*I don't think you can. Your skin has all that protective armour on it.*"

"*Doesn't mean we don't have nerve cells,*" Salanraja said. "*I've never told you this, Bengie, but we dragons have very sensitive skin.*"

"*Ben!*" I said.

"*Fine, Ben . . . Please can you retract your claws a little and also tone down that anxiety. It's already been a long enough day.*"

"*What? How can I stop being anxious? We've lost the battle and we're about to lose the war.*"

"*No,*" Salanraja said. "*We've not lost until we're dead. That's something you've never seemed to grasp. We fight until the last breath.*"

"*But we can't do anything without Asinda . . .*" Then I remembered Salanraja's ability to communicate with other dragons from afar. "*Wait, have you reached out to Shadorow?*"

"*For now, we just need to get to our meeting point, and then we can work things out.*"

"*And when will that be?*" I asked.

"*Soon . . .*"

Just as soon as Salanraja said it, I heard roars from Olan and Corralsa, Aleam's white and Max's black dragon respectively, who being the largest were heading the formation. I climbed up to Salanraja's head to see the two huge dragons begin to turn.

They picked up speed and our formation widened out, with the dwarf dragons being ridden by the cats fanning towards the outside. Salanraja also sped up, and I caught a glimpse of Ishtkar,

Quarl, and Pinacole only a few yards away on the other wing of our formation.

"*What's going on?*" I asked. "*Salanraja . . .*"

"*We've found Asinda,*" Salanraja said. "*She's with the Dragon Guard. They're in battle against the warlocks and they've called for reinforcements.*"

"*What?*"

"*Can you see it?*" Salanraja nodded slightly towards a pinprick of light on the horizon. It brightened as we gathered speed.

"*What is it?*" I asked.

"*The Grand Crystal. The Dragon Guard chased Alliander over the meadows, and they've caught up with her.*"

I squinted my eyes to see shapes flying around it. The vague V shapes of dragons, and something even larger than they. Fire streaked across the sky, and from the battle came sounds like distant thunder.

"*Whiskers,*" I said. I'd thought after our battle with the warlocks and the adventure in the Ghost Realm, we'd at least have an hour or so to have some rest.

I was also worried about my dragon riding students. Through all our adventures since leaving Bestian Academy, they hadn't had a chance to learn how to use their magic. I needed to get them through a portal to the Fifth Dimension, not into another battle.

But then, if we recovered the Grand Crystal, maybe none of this would come to pass.

I could see the facets of the massive crystal now, and I didn't like what I saw. Because a miasma of purple gas surrounded it, making it look like one of the pictures I used to see on television sometimes that telescopes had taken of distant galaxies. The crystal itself was also aglow, and shining with a fusion of bright purple and white light. That meant that someone or something in that battle was using it to cast magic. Given the power that thing held, that couldn't bode well for us at all.

Suddenly, my stomach heaved as I felt Salanraja accelerate to twice her normal speed. The sudden jerk almost sent me tumbling off her head, but I dug my claws into her hide to keep purchase. Salanraja emitted a deep growl, and I knew it wasn't because of her sensitive skin. All around us the other dragons also growled, and many others roared.

"*What is it, Salanraja?*" I asked.

"*We're getting pulled in . . . It's the crystal. It's taken on a power of its own.*"

My hackles went up on the back of my neck. Though my fur was short, I could still feel the wind blowing through it. It found its way underneath my harness, and caused it to puff up like a balloon.

I found myself growling in turn as my eyes focused on that massive glowing crystal, which gained definition as we accelerated. Though I couldn't see them, I could sense invisible sparks of dark magic reaching out to us, pulling us ever closer. Just as when Junas had cast his magic on me before, my muscles felt incredibly weak, and I once again gained that throbbing sensation at the back of my skull.

That's when I heard it: the deep sonorous voice of *Cana Dei*. It hadn't spoken to me inside my mind for a long time, and yet it was there, loud and clear.

"*This is the extent of my power,*" it said, and I realised it wasn't only talking to me but anything in the vicinity that could touch any kind of magic. "*This is just a taste for all of you of how it will all end.*"

From behind the crystal, a massive creature emerged that I could now see clearly against the brightening sky. The beast was bigger than an elephant, bigger than a giraffe, bigger than Matharon had probably been at the peak of his growth. It was hard to judge, given the distance, but I figured it to be about three times the size of the mightiest dragon known to the First Dimension.

But this beast wasn't a dragon; it was a griffin with a huge golden eagle's head, massive feathery wings with thick pinions that looked like writhing boa constrictors, and the powerful hind legs of the strongest of lions. Its forelegs ended in sharp talons, and these gripped the most gigantic staff I'd ever seen.

The shaft was so white in colour that I guessed it to have once been the bole of a birch tree. I say this because affixed to its head was the Grand Crystal in all its intense glory. Alliander had found a way to attach it to a staff and use it at full power.

It turned its head towards us, and I could swear its beady eyes looked right at me. Then it opened its giant beak and from it emerged an incredibly loud and shrill shriek.

19

FIGHT WITH A GRIFFIN

There came another shriek from the sky, and a platoon of bone dragons emerged from the clouds. There were so many of them, spewing acid at the dragons of the King's Dragon Guard who were trying to get close to the griffin. Claws raked, and magic flared from the staffs of the human riders atop all kinds of different dragons. The air smelled of a pungent blend of magic, some of it crisp, some of it acrid, and the stench of rotten vegetable juice dominated over it all.

Down on the ground, another battle raged. The fields and meadows had long given way to scorched earth. Unicorns and regular soldiers on horseback charged with White Magic and swords against hosts of manipulators, golems and gnashing wargs. Archers stood atop the peaks of the hillocks in the distance, sending volleys of arrows into the fray. Foot soldiers in shiny armour had their blue painted shields locked together as they attempted to advance and hack our enemies down.

But though our forces were organised, we didn't seem to be winning the battle. For every soldier we had, there was a magical creation to fight. In places, the manipulators had cast forests of Mandragoras with toothy heads that snapped like massive Venus flytraps at our allies. The whole earth was coated with a blanket of purple mist, getting thicker as the battle raged on. The Grand Crystal also seemed able to cast magic on every single creature on the battlefield, tendrils reaching out through a structure of darkness like mycelium, only visible if you knew it was there. The effect seemed to augment our enemies and sap the strength of our allies. And personally, I just didn't know how to handle it.

Energy not only flowed in narrow lines from the Great Crystal towards any force that assailed the griffin, or the transformed Captain Alliander I should say, but streams of it also flowed into the griffin's feathers and tail. I guess it was this magic that was making the beast so massive, giving Alliander the strength to hold the crystal affixed to the giant birchwood staff in her talons.

"*Summon your staff bearer,*" Salanraja said. "*They need all the help they can get.*"

In truth I was trying, but there was something about the magic that was coming from the Grand Crystal at the end of the griffin Alliander's giant staff. I could sense a stream of dark magic focused directly at me. Though I couldn't hear the voice of *Cana Dei*, I could feel it writhing in my head, tentacles of darkness tickling the grey matter of my brain and sapping my focus. Still there was that same throbbing sensation in my temples, and the muscles in my limbs couldn't move one bit.

"*Ben?*" Salanraja said.

"*I can't . . . It's the magic. It's too powerful.*"

Salanraja growled, her scales rumbling beneath my paws. "*I see . . . The only way through is to work together. Mould your mind to mine.*"

"*What do you mean?*"

Salanraja didn't say anything in reply, at least not immediately.

Instead, I sensed her connecting to my mind, and then I could also feel her pain as the crystal pulled her ever closer. She was trying to flap her wings, to escape the grasp of this unnatural gravity that held her. But instead, it kept her wings held rigid and all she could do was glide towards the crystal. She couldn't move her neck and tail to turn. She could only flap when the crystal, or at least Alliander's magic controlling the crystal, allowed, so as to keep at a constant level. It was as if Alliander had suddenly invented air traffic control.

"*Bengie,*" Salanraja said, sounding ever so slightly frustrated. "*You're not doing it.*"

"*Doing what?*"

"*My mind to yours, and your mind to mine. Didn't you ever listen to Driar Lonamm's lessons on Advanced Dragon Bonding?*"

"*No...*" I said.

I'd been asleep through most of her lessons. Truth be told, in fact, I'd slept through nearly all of the classes in Dragonsbond Academy. But then what did Salanraja expect? I was a *cat*.

My dragon sighed from underneath me, and I knew this because of the brief and narrow jet of flame that came out of her mouth. "*Just work with me to control my body, and I'll work with you to control yours.*"

I really didn't know what she was on about. Honestly, with the way that my head was throbbing at its side, I just couldn't concentrate. "*I don't know—*"

"*Gracious demons, Bengie! Just focus. Your body will work out what to do.*"

By this point she was shouting in my mind, which did exactly what it was intended to do. I could feel her probing through my thoughts, looking for an opening. I'd never truly let her in my head so deep, and I have to admit I was scared.

Meanwhile, we'd flown so close to the Grand Crystal at the

end of Alliander's staff that it now loomed above and beneath us, all the while burning with the power of a thousand suns. Intense waves of heat seemed to blast out from it like invisible solar flares, and as I gazed into its depths, I felt even more drained. Within moments Salanraja would collide with it, ending our bond and both of our lives.

As if feeling my alarm, Salanraja calmed down a little. *"Relax, Ben,"* she said. *"That's all it takes. Close your eyes if it helps."*

I took a deep breath, the pain in my temples making my head feel numb. Then, I closed my eyes as Salanraja had suggested, and all of a sudden, I felt a soothing sensation in my head.

It felt in a way like a warm rain, washing over me after wallowing in mud and letting it dry a little. All the stickiness in my brain just seemed to seep away.

Then, I found myself reaching out for my staff bearer. I didn't do so through thoughts or will of my own; rather I just felt my mind performing the actions, as if it were an external part of my body. The giant white hand appeared from the gaps between worlds and plunged the staff into my mouth, the whole action feeling like an out of body experience.

At the same time, my mind had found its way into Salanraja's body. I could feel her blood flowing along the expanse of it, from head to tail to every single pinion that extended from her wing.

Everything was warmed by the dragonfire burning in her belly. And all the while, I felt rage swelling inside her. Rage at what the great White Mage Alliander had become, and frustration at the ignorant creature of a cat that Salanraja had bonded to.

Fortunately, I was too far removed from my own brain to feel any chagrin over Salanraja's emotions. Rather I focused on what needed to be done.

Salanraja's wings felt cold at their tips, and so I willed extra blood towards them. Simultaneously, I tamped down Salanraja's rage that was fuelling her negative spiral of thoughts. I also curled up Salanraja's wings a little to break the hold on them caused by *Cana Dei*.

Within moments, Salanraja was turning away from the crystal, just as it looked ready to swallow us whole. She beat her wings and dived down towards the ground. A Manipulator saw us approaching and turned its spectral staff towards her, letting out a white beam. But my dragon turned her body just in time and pinwheeled into a half-somersault, and then lifted herself back to join the battle.

A little further along the ground, the five warlocks stood right beneath the Grand Crystal, surrounded by armies of *Cana Dei's* minions. They were so tightly packed together that our forces had no chance of reaching them. Clearly the warlocks had found their way onto the battlefield faster than we had, but then they hadn't had an army of untrained dragon riding cats to slow them down.

They didn't seem so focused on the battle around them, but rather on the Grand Crystal hovering in the air above their heads, held in place by the giant griffin's talons. They had their staffs drawn and the purple crystals on them channelled power into the much larger Grand Crystal. I saw Moonz's pale and cracked face, and I noticed the intensity of the fire burning there.

A shudder went down my spine as realisation washed over me. Their spell was building power inside the Grand Crystal for another huge spell. This was the will of *Cana Dei*.

"I've got an opening!" The voice that belonged to the clarion call coming from close by sounded incredibly familiar. I turned my head to see the fiery long hair of the woman it belonged to, streaking out in all directions as her charcoal dragon dived down towards the warlocks. The dragon rider held a white mage's staff with crystals set along the edge of it, all of them glowing bright white. She had her staff poised ready to cast a disruptive spell into the circle of warlocks.

"*It's Asinda,*" I said to Salanraja. "*She's here.*"

Her dragon, Shadorow, was apparently the fastest dragon in all of the King's forces, and so it made sense for him to break away from the formation. Asinda was also an accomplished mage, with the ability to use both dark and white magic just like Seramina, Esme and me.

For a moment I thought she would stop whatever Alliander was planning. Maybe we could then all work together and over-power the great griffin and retrieve the Grand Crystal. We could stop *Cana Dei* in its tracks once and for all.

But she was already too late . . .

Just as energy started to flow to Asinda's staff, the Grand Crystal also shimmered with a new kind of magic. With a cry of victory, the warlocks beneath us gave one last and victorious thrust, and a massive shockwave pulsed out of the Grand Crystal at the end of Alliander's mighty staff.

None of us knew what had hit us. One moment we were flying on our dragons, or charging on our steeds, or had bows nocked or shields locked, approaching the enemy slowly but surely. The next, a massive wave of force had washed over us, powerful enough to render even the mightiest of dragons inert and send them plummeting from the sky.

I saw sparks, then blotches, and then Salanraja's control gave way beneath me. Together, we plummeted towards the ground.

20

THE BEGINNING OF THE END

There was only darkness and the sensation of falling. Gravity pulled at the fur on my face, set my cheeks wobbling, and caused my stomach to churn.

For a moment I thought we were going to die, but I quickly came to my senses. I'd been in this situation too many times when I'd closed my eyes and tried to escape imminent death. It was better to face whatever was coming head on.

Just before we hit the ground, I opened my eyes and saw that Salanraja had managed to unfurl her wings at the very last moment. She jerked, then steadied herself into a glide, but it wasn't enough to stop her underbelly from crashing into the ground.

Dirt scuffed up around her, some of it smacking me in the face hard. I felt a sharp sting and I tasted grit. The pain sealed my eyes shut once again.

I couldn't move, and it felt like it would take all the strength in the world to pry my eyes open. It was like that moment in nightmares that you know you want to wake up, but your body doesn't let you, and all you need to do is to lift yourself onto your legs, to open your eyes, and—

Light flooded my vision. I could see the Grand Crystal hovering above me, clutched in the staff held by the claws of the mighty griffin that had once been Alliander. A large beam of purple light led up to the crystal from the ground, the effect of the convergence of the warlocks' magic from their own staffs. The sky now had been almost completely cleared of dragons. Other than the few still falling from the sky, the only creatures that didn't lie inert were the five warlocks and the griffin.

Their powerful magic had taken down even our enemy's forces. But it didn't matter, because soon it was all going to end. Once every few seconds or so, the crystal let off a kind of shockwave, just like the one that had knocked us all out of the sky. And with each pulse, I felt a new wave of weakness that sent pain shuddering through my muscles, making me writhe over the ground. It was unbearable. I just wanted it to end, and I could feel in Salanraja's mind that she felt exactly the same way.

There was no space for thought. No space for comforting or to be comforted by my dragon. No space to flee or to transform into a chimera and try to charge the warlocks in between pulses. There was only wave after wave of debilitating weakness. Now there was absolutely no way we could win.

I'm not sure where it came from – it might have been through the dark magic of the crystal, or it might have come from the griffin's mouth. But the voice of *Cana Dei* boomed across the sky in a terrifying baritone, sending shudders down my weakened spine.

"You have made this so easy," it said. "The greatest of your forces all brought together. Here I can end you all, and then I can take all the time I want to unite the worlds. Rejoice, foolish creatures of the light, for the era of eternal darkness will come to pass sooner than even I imagined. Behold, the beginning of the end."

The beam that the warlocks were sending up into the crystal became ever brighter. The shockwaves came faster and faster, and the weakness became even more intense. Eventually, I couldn't even feel the muscles in my paws.

It seemed as if there was no way out. As *Cana Dei* had so aptly put it, we were about to die.

21

AID AND SACRIFICE

Just when it seemed we were about die, aid came during the darkest of waves. It started as a pinprick of light only yards away from the warlocks. Then it grew to a circle, and expanded even further vertically until it was a great yawning portal into another land.

I saw warm darkness on the other side, and faint pink outlines, and then I made out the shape of a massive black cat, shaped slightly like a panther, wearing a golden torc around its neck.

I chirped with delight, because I could think of no one else I wanted to see at that moment. Bastet had opened the portal. Just as we had reached the precipice of defeat, she had decided to send aid.

Familiar shrieks filled our surroundings, and thousands of flying creatures swarmed out into the empty sky. These fabled guardians of the Fifth Dimension were known as aeriosaurs, with wings like bats and beaks like buzzards, and were impossible to kill with anything but pure dark magic. The magic coming off the

Grand Crystal didn't seem to be of this variety, and so the shock-waves didn't seem to affect them.

Like crows getting ready to feed on a fallen deer, they swarmed together into a ball in the sky. Within this they turned, their momentum building towards the warlocks and they formed into one straight line like an iron girder sailing across the sky.

The warlocks looked up at the approaching force, and they must have realised they had no choice. If they didn't break away the energy that they were directing into the Grand Crystal, then the aeriosaurs would rip them to shreds and tatters with their sharp beaks.

The beam that they were casting upwards broke, and instead they twisted and spun their staffs around in unnaturally fluid motions. Out of the five warlocks' crystals came a succession of quickfire purple rays. Each of them had short enough bursts of power to bring down the attacking swarm of aeriosaurs.

Aeriosaurs were the defenders of the Fifth Dimension, protectors of the realm where the souls of all living creatures reside. They could only be defeated by dark magic, and this came against them with such intense force that within moments the swarm was just settling feathers and dust.

Bastet had clearly sent them out knowing that they'd be sacrificed, and this had certainly bought enough time for strength to return to my muscles. I lifted myself on all fours, my back and thighs shaking as I stretched. I turned towards the portal to see Bastet looking out at us, about to speak. Her voice trilled through the air, like a mixture of tinkling wind chimes and the soft Welsh accent that my former mistress used to use in South Wales. It came as if from all directions, as if the clouds and the weather were speaking to us through the very fabric of space time.

"All of you who are meant to come to my realm, may now do so," she said. "For those who have seen the prophecies know if they are destined to attend my court. The rest of you should retreat. Save this battle for another day, because today you will find yourself at an impasse."

There came a rumbling and deep laughter from the Grand Crystal, that went completely black for a moment, seeming to suck in the light from all around it. Tendrils of darkness lashed out from it, and out came the sonorous voice of *Cana Dei*.

"You must take me for a fool, Bastet," it said. "For now, you have lost the defenders of your realm, and I shall soon find my way into it too."

As *Cana Dei* spoke, the warlocks had already found enough time to raise their staffs and start the magic that would once again feed the Grand Crystal's debilitating spell. Clearly we had only moments to respond, and that wouldn't be enough time for everyone whom Bastet had called upon to get through her portal.

In reply to *Cana Dei's* retort, out of Bastet's throat and from every single molecule around us that could emit sound, came a growl so powerful that it could only belong to a feline goddess. "Corporal Lars and brave Camillan. You have both seen the visions in your dreams, and you know what you must do."

I turned around to see Asinda, standing only several spine-spans away from me now. Her eyes had gone wide, and she managed to move her jaw enough to utter the word, "Lars?"

I spun around to follow her gaze. When we'd all fallen, one dragon with its rider had fallen close enough to warlocks to make a difference.

Out of the purple crystals strewn across the ground that once had been an army of magical creations, a citrine dragon emerged. It roared into the sky, a powerful column of flame spewing out from its mouth in front of it.

Though Camillan, Lars' dragon, would have known she couldn't defeat the massive griffin whom she charged towards, she didn't seem to care. Alliander seemed to register surprise, then she turned towards the dragon her giant beak, poised and ready to snap her in two. But Camillan was faster and barrelled right into her chest. The impact was so great and so charged with fire, that it knocked the staff from the griffin's talons. There came a flurry of feathers, a great snapping sound and my mind completely blacked out what had happened to Lars' dragon – I have no memory of it. Let's just say it wasn't pretty.

Camillan's body tumbled lifeless from the sky.

The griffin didn't waste any time either, and swooped down straight after the staff and caught it up in its talons. As the yellow dragon fell, the griffin brought the staff and crystal back to its original position, looking as if nothing had distracted it at all.

"Lars! What are you doing, you idiot!" The cry had come from Asinda, who had now moved closer to me.

I looked back to see that she wasn't focused on the battle in the sky. Rather, she watched her boyfriend, the young man who had once been High Prefect in Dragonsbond Academy. The famous hero who was so skilled with shield magic and so courageous that he'd risen through the ranks when he entered the Dragon Guard, being the first dragon rider to become corporal in only a few months. Lars, whom we all respected. The young man whom the girls all had loved in Dragonsbond Academy and the boys had all wanted to be.

"Lars!" Asinda shouted again. "Stop!"

He was charging towards the warlocks, his staff with the white crystal on it in his hand. The warlocks, who were so focused on getting the magic ready to stream back into the crystal, didn't notice his approach. He didn't utter a cry, but I can imagine his boots trudged loudly over the crystals scattered around him. But still he ran, and at the same time lifted his staff up high, and it started to glow.

Lars knew shield magic, which meant he could cast a barrier of kinetic energy that could stop most magic in its tracks. I'd heard rumours, in fact, that he was the strongest shield magician to have entered the king's forces in the last two hundred years.

The warlocks turned towards him, but they had moved far too late. The crystal at the end of his staff was already glowing bright white. He used the strength in his shoulder to throw himself right into the centre of the warlocks. Then, a magical dome of pure kinetic energy fountained out of his staff, enveloping himself and the five warlocks. At exactly the same time, the magical beams shot out of their five staffs, heading to a focal point that would have converged the magic on the Grand Crystal had Lars' magical shield not blocked it.

The magic hit the inner ceiling of the shield, then it bounced back onto the earth as one large beam, and dissipated, knocking both Lars and the warlocks to the ground.

22

ESCAPE

"Lars!" Asinda called for a second time, and she started to run towards her ever faithful boyfriend. But her charcoal dragon Shadorow stepped forward to block her path.

From the other side of the portal to the Fifth Dimension, Bastet regarded her for a moment. "Come," she said. "We have little time."

I could see that the cats had already joined Bastet. Seramina aboard Hallinar was on the way, just about passing the threshold when I noticed her.

Several other dragons followed in her wake, namely Olan with Aleam, Ishtkar with Rine, Quarl with Ange, Kada with Ta'ra, Gratis with Esme, Corralsa with Max, and Salanraja by herself.

"Come on Bengie," my dragon said in my mind. *"We cannot delay any longer."*

I considered the portal. I knew that we needed Asinda on the other side. Bastet had told me that much, and I didn't want to mess with fate. I walked up to the red haired dragon rider, who was struggling to try and get past Shadorow.

"We need to go to the Fifth Dimension," I said to her. "Bastet said we need you there."

She had her teeth clenched and was staring at her boyfriend across the battlefield. "I'm not going without Lars."

As if they'd understood Bastet perfectly, the unicorns were already in retreat, sending up dust in their wake. The King's Dragon Guard were also mounted on their dragons, heading back towards Cimlean City. This battle clearly wasn't in their favour today.

"We don't have a choice," I said. "Lars wouldn't want you to die here."

"No . . ." Asinda said. "He's not dead."

I turned back to look at him. I could already see the warlocks standing up. Lars wasn't getting up. If he wasn't dead, he was unconscious on the ground, and by the way that the warlocks were pointing their staffs at him – the fire burning at the back of their eyes – that coma wouldn't last for long.

"We need to—"

"No," Asinda snapped back, and she crossed her arms. "I told you I'm not going without him, and you can't do anything to change my mind."

She tried to sidestep around Shadorow, who was watching her with his yellow eyes. As soon as Asinda moved, Shadorow also did, to block her. He wasn't going to let her charge to her doom, breaking the bond between woman and dragon.

Meanwhile, we had mere seconds, and I had no chance of moving her as a normal cat. Already, the griffin in the sky had turned its staff around and the crystal would soon be pointing at us.

I realised that Shadorow could pick her up in his mouth and carry her into the Fifth Dimension, but he seemed hesitant. Perhaps he didn't want to do something that she might never forgive, or perhaps he didn't quite understand how important it was for Asinda to be there.

"I have no choice," I muttered under my breath, and I willed into my muscles the power of the second gift my crystal had given me all those months ago.

It was the fastest that I'd ever transformed, and the pain was even more intense than I'd ever experienced it. My muscles tore and burst, a head grew out of my neck, and horns out of that. My tail transformed into a snake and my head into a lion, and my front legs and back hoofs became much more powerful than those of mere Bengal.

Before Asinda even had time to realise what I was up to, I lowered my goat head and with all the force in my back hoofs, I rammed her into the Fifth Dimension.

Behind me, Shadorow grunted. Through the way he displayed his sharp yellowing teeth, he looked as if he were about to tear me in two. I was big as a chimera, but he was bigger and no doubt stronger too.

Behind him, power had started to grow in the staff in Alliander's talons. The air smelled of charred earth and rotten vegetable juice. Distantly, I could hear the flapping and pounding of retreating dragons, horses, unicorns and soldiers.

Fury burned in the griffin's eyes, then a beam came out of its staff. My heart jumped in my chest, because it was aimed at Shadorow and looked as if it would disintegrate him. But he had already bounded through the portal. The beam hit the empty spot on the ground where he'd been standing, sending up the smell of charred soil.

Alliander turned the beam towards me, and I could feel the heat pulling on my fur. I didn't waste a moment; I bounded through the portal.

Just before it closed behind me, I turned back to see the beams of destructive dark magic surge out of the warlocks' staffs, all of them focused on Lars who lay supine on the ground.

23

ANGER AND DESPAIR

I'd been warned many times back in Dragonsbond Academy about the dangers of alteration magic, or in other words transforming into other creatures. If you stayed in your target form for too long, or you transformed too many times into it, there was a risk you'd become that creature permanently.

As anyone reading this would already be aware, I was proud to be a Bengal. Also, despite the mighty lion's head and paws, I didn't particularly like having a goat's head growing out of my neck and a snake growing out of my tail. I had nightmares sometimes of transforming into a chimera and never being able to turn back again. Honestly, I think that's why I'd started to use this ability less and less.

So, as you can imagine, as soon as the portal from the First to the Fifth dimension sealed shut behind me, and I knew we were safe, I willed my body to become Bengal again.

The transformation wasn't as easy as I'd hoped. It hurt even more to transform back than it had to transform into a chimera. My bones creaked and my muscles felt as if they were clinching in on each other, squashing themselves in unnatural ways. I roared and I growled and I yowled. It was only when I emitted a soft meow that I let out a breath of relief, because this was a sound that neither lions, goats, nor snakes could make.

I was in the Fifth Dimension, which I knew reasonably well because I'd visited this realm a couple of times before. Everything here was almost completely black except the pink glowing outlines where the forms of objects turned, giving them definition. I could hear no sound of aeriosaurs in the sky. Bastet must have sent the last of them against the warlocks.

What I could see was Asinda standing right above me, glaring down at me with her narrowed cornflower eyes. I could see only rage on the hard edges of her face, flecked with tears that had already been cried. She held her staff tightly in her hands, but none of the crystals on it were aglow. Instead, she wielded it like a human might wield a hockey stick in the Fourth Dimension, and it looked right now like she was considering me as a puck.

"You!" she said to me, her lips trembling. "You stopped me. I could have helped him, or at least . . ."

I wanted to reach out and be sympathetic, but after that battle I had no patience whatsoever. "Or what?" I asked. "You would have gone after him and sacrificed yourself? What use would you have been in the battles to come then?"

"I," – she stopped herself even before she could start the sentence – "I don't know what I would have done. But you have no right to make my decisions for me."

"We need you here!" I screamed, or perhaps yowled, back. "We've seen prophecies, and we were meant to bring you here. It's the only way we can stop the destruction of the worlds."

"I don't want to do anything without Lars," Asinda said. She glared over her shoulder at Bastet. "Open the portal. Send me back. I can still save him . . . Or if he's . . . I belong with him, not here with all of you."

At that, Shadorow who was standing right beside Salanraja opened his mouth and roared. Clearly, they'd also been having an argument about all this in their heads.

"So what are you going to do?" I asked, cocking my head at her staff. "Hit me with your stick and send me to the other side of the realm? Or maybe you want me to turn into a chimera again so you can battle something that looks like a monster."

Asinda's eyes narrowed even more. The way she held her staff, it looked like she really did want to use it.

"Just leave the Dragoncat alone," came a voice from my side.

At first I thought it must be Ta'ra. But she didn't speak in such a whiny male voice, and she also wouldn't tend to address a human in the cat language. Instead, to my surprise, the ratty King of Cats of Cimlean City stepped in front of me. He continued to speak in the cat language at Asinda, not seeming to care that she just wouldn't understand.

"This Dragoncat here is a hero," he said. "I saw what he did. He turned into a mighty creature like I've never seen him do before. And if he didn't bring you here, you'd be dead now, you hear? You should be grateful, you whiny human thing."

To me, it sounded like a powerful diatribe, but to Asinda it must have sounded like a sequence of growls and yowls. She cast her narrow gaze upon Rex, her nostrils flared. But she said nothing.

"Will you two give the girl a break," said another voice from behind me. Ta'ra. "She's just lost someone very dear to her. She doesn't need lecturing right now. She needs some time alone."

Ta'ra strolled by me, her tail raised as an indication that she approached in peace. For the first time in a long time, she'd decided not to take my side on something. Instead, she curled around Asinda's leg, and sat there quietly, the only sounds coming out of her body being a rhythmic and mournful purr.

Max also came around from behind Asinda, and he whined softly, and then curled himself around her other leg. Asinda looked down at both of them, the grip on her staff loosening. She continued to stare down Rex, but the harshness had begun to dissolve in her gaze.

Seramina then floated in from the side. She had her arms open, her staff now fastened to her back. Her chiffon dress bunched up over her arms as she accepted Asinda into her embrace.

"Seramina, please," Asinda said. "Can you open a portal back? Lars is . . ." She didn't seem to have the strength to finish the sentence.

"I'm sorry, Asinda," Seramina said. "Lars would want you to be safe."

"But he's—"

"There's nothing you can do. Lars would want you to stay safe."

"I . . ." Asinda left the thought incomplete. Instead, she melted into Seramina's hug, shuddering as she did so. I didn't see her cry, but I smelled her tears.

And that, I guessed, was the difference between being a human and a cat. Humans knew how to handle these things, while all we cats could do was just sit there and wonder how long it would be until our next meal.

✣ 24 ✣

WAKING

In the Fifth Dimension, there's no way of measuring day and night. There's no sunshine there, only the magic that outlines the realm in pink and provides it with warmth. I slept on a soft bed that felt a little like hay and smelled like it too. All of us cats slept on these, along with Max who rested somewhere among us. I couldn't see him, but I could hear his panting and his soft snores.

There was a hut on the island, difficult to discern from the darkness unless you knew what to look for. The humans slept in there in rooms of their own, with their own beds and reading lights. But – and not only because I couldn't read – I decided I'd rather sleep out in the open air.

Partly this was because I didn't want any more run-ins with Asinda; I just didn't know how to handle her right now. Also, I wanted to prove myself as a cat amongst cats. I wanted them to understand that they could learn to be just like me, the great Dragoncat, but alas, none of them had the honour of being descendants of the great Asian leopard cat. But each of them had unique qualities of his or her own.

The dragons also slept outside, but they had chosen to gather by themselves, and Salanraja wasn't up yet. I could hear her mumbling inside my mind in the language of her dreams, but it was all nonsense, so I didn't pay any heed to it.

Ta'ra was nestled next to me, and she didn't stir when I lifted myself up on all fours. But when I took a few steps away, she mumbled in the cat language, "Ben? Where are you going?"

"I'm going to find some breakfast."

"Just a little a longer," Ta'ra said. "I don't feel like I've slept an hour."

"Sleep as long as you like." And I walked off, turning my ears so I could listen to the rhythm of her soft breathing.

Though Bastet had mentioned training all the cats when she'd met us in the Ghost Realm, she had expressed no urgency in starting immediately. She seemed to understand that we needed time for rest and recovery.

She'd set us up on the island in the centre of the River of Souls, which ran all the way from an indefinite source to the Final Falls at the end of it all that ultimately tumbled into the void, also known as the Eighth Dimension. The river meandered through a canyon, with niches inset into each wall that contained lanterns full of pink wisps of light. These were the souls of every living creature across all the dimensions, and Bastet's job alongside her feline sons and daughters was to protect these.

The souls glowed in their lanterns, casting sparkles over the dark flowing waters, dancing with the rhythm of the currents like fireflies through eternal dark. It was the first time I'd noticed, but some of these lanterns contained two pink wisps, both of them dancing around each other. This certainly struck me as strange. Was it possible for a creature to have two souls?

The air here had a scent like honey, everything sweet and comforting. My tummy was rumbling, I was so hungry. This wasn't just because of the previous battle; somehow I always was after transforming into a chimera and back again. I had a theory that the food in my stomach didn't expand when I turned into a chimera but did shrink when I transformed back again. Though I wasn't sure that Bastet would have any food for us.

I was proven wrong, because bowls of cat food had been placed out in rows of about twenty, each of them containing what looked like particularly moist tuna. I meowed as I approached one, and I wolfed it down as if I still had a lion's mouth. I'd been so hungry that I'd not realised which cat was eating from the bowl next me. I turned to see Rex looking at me, licking his lips, displaying a fine pair of sharp, tiny teeth.

"So what's today, boss?" he asked.

"Boss?" I asked. I cocked my head and looked at him askance.

"Yeah . . . Why, aren't you our boss?"

"I'm not sure," I admitted. "Meanwhile, here I was thinking that you were the king of all the cats in Cimlean City. Doesn't that make you the boss?"

"Well, I am a king," Rex said. "But you're the mighty Dragoncat, with the power to turn into that massive lion thing. If I'd known you could do that, I would never have shown you disrespect."

"Is this some form of apology?" I asked, and I took a sniff of his tail.

"I don't know about that. I've never had to do any of that apologising stuff before, and don't intend to start now. Anyway, are we going to start training today? Because I want to learn to use my staff. I think all of the cats do after what we saw today."

"I don't know," I said. "You'll have to talk to Bastet."

Rex looked behind him to where the Manx, Geni, and the Persian, Bruno, sat waiting. He turned back to me. "It's just, I did. Bastet told me to come see you, you see. She said that you'll be showing us how it's done. I mean, maybe I could learn to transform into one of those massive three headed beasts, just like you . . ."

"It's called a chimera," I said. "And your crystal needs to gift you with the ability to turn into one, which I believe is very rare."

"Is it now? Chimera, aye . . . That's a good name for a three headed beast. Anyway, my brother, Bruno, here has all the other cats asking when they will meet their unicorns. They're a bit wary about bonding with magical horses, and I'm sure you'll know why."

"I do," I said. I've waxed poetic so often about the untrustworthy nature of horses that I see no need to repeat myself here.

"It's just, I thought, Dragoncat, that maybe you had some answers. When do we start to learn how to use magic properly, and when will our brothers and sisters in the city meet their unicorns that they're talking so much about?"

In all honesty I had absolutely no idea, but I wanted to appear confident in front of Rex. Call it a tomcat thing, if you like. At the same time, I felt anything but assured. Last time I had tried to lead these cats, I had had it backfire on me. They were still hoping for something that I wasn't sure I could give.

"I'm guessing I'm going to need to talk to Bastet first," I said and I sauntered off, leaving the Cimlean City trio to work out what to do next amongst themselves.

25

ON LEADERSHIP

I had to move away from the island's shore to find Bastet. She'd secluded herself in a cave with walls so textured that they looked to have a colour of their own. She sat with her head craned high, the pink light from the walls playing patterns in the reflections on her shiny torc. She wasn't alone, being engaged in conversation with the golden blonde-haired teenager, Bellari.

At first, I thought I'd go and interrupt them, but something about Bellari's rigid posture told me they didn't want to be disturbed. So instead, I turned my ears towards them and listened in while I gave myself a good groom.

"It's beautiful here," Bellari said. "I can't believe that just a year ago none of us even knew about the Fifth Dimension, and now the way that the pink light plays off the darkness, and the smell of this place, just makes me want to stay here forever."

"You already know that that isn't possible," Bastet said. "This realm is only for those that protect souls."

Bastet was in fact referring to the cats who had lived here for a long time and spent the days scouring for ways that *Cana Dei* was trying to enter the realm. It had ways of finding its own ways in, sending rats, snakes and scorpions from the Ghost Realm through temporary portals so they could try to find rifts in the fabric of space-time. There were holes in here, apparently, that *Cana Dei* could exploit and meander its way towards the souls, destroying all life by erasing their very cores of existence. The cats, who were biologically immortal in this realm where time didn't pass as it normally did, spent their days hunting such creatures and hence keeping *Cana Dei* at bay.

"I know I can't stay here . . ." Bellari, said and she lowered her head. "I don't want to, really. I just want to be able to settle down and have children and – you know. I want to live a good life. I want for Rine and me to be happy, after we have time to marry that is. He has so many plans for a wedding, and I want us to at least have a good one. Is that too much to ask?"

"And that is why you fight?" Bastet asked. "In the hope that those things will come to pass?"

"And that is why I fight," Bellari said. "But can we win? I mean, I know that you brought us here so we can have a chance. Yet still, Rine and me, and Ange as well. I don't think any of us really believe."

I found myself growling at that, and then I caught myself. After all, Bellari had been nice to me before, so maybe she wasn't so bad. Maybe she and Rine could visit me in my retirement fortress sometimes, so long as Seramina or Ange invited her and she didn't start any of her allergy nonsense again.

"Your future is . . ." Bastet trailed off as if thinking about what to say.

"What is it?" Bellari asked.

Bastet took a deep breath. I'd never seen her so concerned before. "High Prefect Bellari, I believe that you've been taking extra lessons with Great Driar Yila."

Great Driar Yila was one of the Council of Three, the over-seers in Dragonsbond Academy. Though the aging and lithe woman had first seemed strict and harsh, I'd later discovered her to be an incredibly loyal and courageous person. She was like the other two members of the Council of Three – protectors of us all.

"I have," Bellari said.

"And has she taught you the ultimate fire magic?"

This time it was Bellari's turn to hesitate. When she spoke again, her voice had softened and had become laced with fear. "She has . . . but she also said she'd never had to use it. She'd never wish that upon anyone. Neither would I."

"But you know she would use it in a heartbeat if it would protect those around her."

"I do . . ."

Bastet moved closer to Bellari, and she lowered her long neck until her head was level with the young fire mage's face. "Most think of fire as a destructive force, but sometimes what the fire sweeps away creates soil so rich that it allows life to be born anew."

"I remember that from my lessons . . . But wait . . . Are you telling me that I might have to use the magic?"

"You might," Bastet said. "You will know when and if it's time."

"I—I don't want to . . ."

All of a sudden Bellari's face went red, as if she had remem-bered she was 'allergic' to cats, and just precisely while talking to the largest cat in all the dimensions. I can understand how some humans might be allergic to cats, with all our hair and dander and whatnot. But I doubted very much she would react the same way to a feline goddess. After all, I was pretty sure that Bastet didn't moult.

Bastet let out a soft chirp that seemed to soothe Bellari. I had no idea what magical spell they were talking about, but I somehow figured I didn't want to find out.

"I'm just scared," Bellari said.

"That's understandable," Bastet said. "Just remember from now on that you have a perfect right to be afraid."

Suddenly, I heard a cough from behind me, and I spun around to see Aleam standing there. He held his staff propped against the ground, holding his weight. He wore a brown robe with a weathered yellow cloak trailing over the earth.

"Just because you're a hero," he said, "doesn't mean it's a good idea to eavesdrop."

"Aleam," I said. "I just came to ask Bastet what to do next. I saw her talking to Bellari, and I thought I'd better not disturb them."

"Did you now?" Aleam asked, one eyebrow raised. There was an air of accusation in his voice.

"It's not like that," I said. "I've recently realised that Bellari isn't so bad. I mean she was horrible to me, and she was horrible to a lot of people. But she turned out okay in the end. You know, she might even be good for Rine."

Though Aleam's lips curled only slightly, I could see the smile in his eyes. "There aren't really any *bad* people," he said. "There are only the dark consequences that come from those who fear too much. But it's how people deal with that fear over time that defines them as either a hero or villain. And even villains can become better over time if they learn to fear less."

"People, and cats . . ." I said, remembering.

Aleam nodded. "I guess you're referring to that bout you had with *Cana Dei.*"

"It wanted to use fear to make me destroy Seramina. To sacrifice myself to the darkness by making me think there was no point in trying to hope."

"That's how *Cana Dei* works," Aleam said. "And that's how villainy also works in every single story I've been told. The propagation of fear . . . it works like a virus. Fear spreads from one to another, and soon an entire society has caught the bug. That's what *Cana Dei* hopes to achieve. But we can either let the fear control us, or we can embrace hope. And hope . . . well, that's the stuff of heroes."

I meowed, expressing my agreement in a way I thought Aleam would understand. I caught a whiff of Bellari's catnip perfume that she'd borrowed off Ange floating upon a warm breeze. For a moment the air held silence, though if I listened hard enough, I could hear the sounds of snoring dragons from beyond the mouth of the cave.

"So what did you want to ask Bastet?" Aleam asked.

"It was just that Rex told me that I was meant to take them through training today. But I just don't think I'm leader material, Aleam. Rex should be the one leading armies. He is the King of Cats after all. And me . . . I'm not cut out for all this."

"I see," Aleam said. He leaned to one side on his staff and his gaze went distant as if thinking.

"What is it?"

"Didn't you once believe that you would never be able to ride dragons? And then you believed that you'd never use magic. Then you believed that you could never learn to like that dog, Max."

"I did," I said. "But this is different."

"Is it? Because I was just thinking . . . I guess leadership is what I talked about, but on a higher level." He studied me, then seemed to notice the blank expression on my face. After humans have spent enough time with cats, they seem to learn how to read us better. "Think of it this way: it's your job as a leader to get others to forget about their fear, to replace the propagation of fear with the propagation of hope. To give those who have the disease the cure."

"So they won't be scared anymore?"

"No . . . Not like that. You can't eliminate fear; you can only pretend it's not there for a while. Or acknowledge it and carry on regardless."

"I don't understand," I said, remembering my fight with Rex in the Versta Caverns. But hadn't just been a fight – Rex had really been standing up for all the other cats because none of them had believed in what I believed in. They'd just wanted to be cats and they hadn't seen the point in fighting for a greater cause. I had once felt exactly the same way.

"How can I get the others to feel any differently?" I asked.

Aleam chuckled. "That is the magic of it. You don't overthink it, you just do it, and others follow. Once you have enough courage inside, you will find a way."

"I guess I understand," I said, though I said it lightly.

"Do you?" Aleam asked.

In all honesty, I wasn't sure. I'd often thought that pep talks with humans always ended up with the advice that you'd just know what to do when the time came. But what if you didn't know? What if the 'magic' never arrived?

I didn't have a chance to answer Aleam, because Bellari and Bastet had finished their conversation. Bellari walked past Aleam and me. She gave him a meek smile, and then she turned her gaze down to me holding that smile. Her eyelids were flecked with tears that she'd been clearly trying not to let fall. Behind her perfume, I could smell fear, and lots of it at that.

Bastet turned towards me. "Come, Dragoncat," she said. "Let me tell you exactly what you need to know."

26

CATS CAN RIDE UNICORNS TOO

By the time we'd returned to our camp, all the cats were awake. Bellari and Aleam had already entered their hut for some extra sleep. I don't know what had awoken them in the first place; I hadn't even thought to ask. The rest of the humans, the dragons, and Max were still fast aslumber.

Meanwhile, the cats upon waking had instinctively known to follow Bastet. I guessed our bodies still thought it the middle of the night – the time in other words that we usually awoke to have our regular exercise. The humans of the Fourth Dimension had a name for this – the *zoomies*. My ancestors, the great Asian leopard cats of legend, would probably have hunted around this time, when every single cat I knew liked to spend a good hour charging over anything we could find, scratching, climbing, and leaping over obstacles. It was just one of the ways we kept ourselves agile and strong.

As a result, we were naturally restless while Bastet led us over the trail towards the unicorns. Our tails twitched, and every so often one of us would charge ahead of our clowder and then dart around to re-join us. Occasionally, a magical butterfly would flitter by, and then we'd be leaping over each other to catch it. Bastet didn't seem to mind, though. She understood that this was all part of being a cat.

Every one of us had recently discarded our leather harnesses, removed by the humans. We had no need for them anymore, since it was much warmer here than it had been in the Crystal Mountains of the First Dimension.

Our leader guided us over the rolling hills of the Fifth Dimension, the only light coming from the outlines of the shapes of the land and nature, a light that was bright enough to show us the way. It was often hard to discern one landmark from the rest, at least visually. But the land still provided a variety of natural smells – pollen, forest loam, pine and rock all mingled together.

It must have been a good hour's hike up and down, sometimes with the underbrush seeming so thick that I worried one of us would get lost as we wove our way through it. Other times, we found ourselves running over open fields, our energy not seeming to dwindle at all. It wasn't long before we reached our target, and the unicorns were waiting for us.

They'd gathered in a kind of paddock on a plateau above the River of Souls, which we could hear roaring in the distance. I say kind of, because though the paddock had fences, they were magical in construction and the unicorns could pass through the barrier easily if they so chose. Inside the pink outlined fences were stalks of fresh smelling grass. The ground was dewy and soaked my paws to walk over it, but I didn't mind. I've said it many times – I'm of one of those cat breeds that don't mind water.

There was a strong scent of pollen in the air, richer than the usual scents of this realm. It was as if the turf in front of us were full of daisies and poppies and buttercups and dandelions. It didn't take me long to find the outlines of the flowers, enriching the sward on which the unicorns munched.

During my conversation with Bastet, she'd made it clear that before I even trained the dragon riding cats in the use of magic, the street cats of Cimlean City needed to bond with their unicorns. All of them, that is, except Rex and Geni, who were now bonded with a citrine and a ruby dwarf dragon respectively.

Hence, the unicorns had been expecting us. We sauntered into view, my muscles and no doubt those of every one of us except Bastet a little tired from our exertive hike. Bastet turned in front of the paddock and waited.

Ahead the unicorns whinnied, and I caught a sudden whiff of horse. Alas, I'd promised Bastet that I'd be on my best behaviour despite my distaste for the creatures. I needed to help the street cats of Cimlean City believe that they could be proud of bonding with their unicorns. To save the worlds, they needed to accept that just like the humans they'd watched from the rooftops every day, marching through the city on unicornback, they too could be White Mages.

"Come, those that must lead," Bastet said.

Her golden eyes turned first towards Esme, who had agreed to show the new cats the ways of White Magic. Esme strolled forwards, her whole spine swaying with the motion of her hips. She kept her head up high as she approached Bastet, and then turned, her bright blue eyes catching the light.

Bastet's gaze then turned upon me, and a reluctant growl came to me unbidden. But just as soon as the sound started to surface, I stamped it down. I was meant to show these cats how to fight, not how to resist. I was meant to set an example.

I strolled forward, making every step of mine seem as powerful as it possibly could.

"I'm proud of you, Ben," Ta'ra said, and her voice trailed in my wake.

I tried to remember how I had seen my great Asian leopard cat ancestors walk that time in the Ghost Realm and willed my body to stalk forwards in the same hunterly fashion. But after a few steps I felt a little awkward, so instead I mirrored the motion of my father, the mighty George. This seemed much more natural. I heard chirps of appreciation from the cats behind me. They had certainly gained respect for me since they'd seen me turn into a chimera, but that didn't stop me feeling like a bit of an imposter.

Despite my doubts, I kept my head as high as possible. As I turned, I hoped the cats standing before me saw my eyes glinting, just like Esme's had.

Within the crowd, my gaze fell upon Ta'ra first, who gave me a couple of slow blinks to tell me how much she appreciated me. Then I saw Rex, his eyes wide in fascination and locked not upon me but on the great and mighty Bastet. The Cornish Rex for most of his life had never believed that she existed, but now she stood tall and awesome before him, the protector of us all. There was Geni too, and Bruno, and all the other cats gazing upon the three of us with utmost respect. We certainly had their attention. Now we only needed to prove that they could become as capable as the humans.

"To my right, as you know, stands Esme of the White," Bastet said. "Known to some as Magecat, and a daughter who has made me proud." I studied Geni for signs of jealousy but didn't see any. "Esme will teach the cats of Cimlean City how to ride unicorns, just as she once rode one herself." My ears perked up and I turned to Esme in surprise. All that time she'd claimed to be my *companion* and she'd never told me that. I wondered if Rex knew. "She will teach you how to ride a unicorn, how to respect their wishes, and how to channel your power alongside theirs to cast powerful creation magic. The White might have lost the good

Captain Alliander to the darkness, but it will now gain you as capable allies. Now, my daughter, I shall pass the mantle to you."

Bastet looked down at Esme. The Abyssinian's whiskers twitched, and she sniffed the air with her pink nose. The way that the light shone out of the ground all around her suffused her alabaster fur with a warm glow, making her seem like a creature of legend. For a moment, I regretted abandoning her as a *companion* so that I could spend more time with Ta'ra. But what was I thinking? Esme and I just weren't meant to be.

Esme took a step forwards, then she spoke out in a loud voice that was picked up and amplified by a sudden flurry of wind. "The first task," she said. "Is for each of you to bond with your unicorns. You must approach and mount within seconds, and then must stay on as they gallop. Your body will either mould to their form or the unicorn will reject you. Should the latter happen, you will be sent back to the Fifth Dimension as you will have proven yourself unworthy for the cause. I hope that will not happen to any of us here."

It sounded a bit harsh, but I guess if I had fallen off Salanraja on our first flight, I wouldn't have had the luxury of being sent home – as much I'd wanted to be at the time. Instead, I would have been a pancake on the fields outside of Dragonsbond Academy, soon to become a meal for the crows.

There was a flash of light, and Esme's staff bearer appeared with her staff clutched in its tight fist. It placed the staff in her mouth, and the crystals along the staff's length were suffused with a cool light. Wispy stalks floated out of her staff, converging to a point beneath the white Abyssinian's paws.

The wisps then started to spin around and around in a horizontal circle, buoying Esme up until she was hovering in the air. Her eyes were now bright white, filled with the same magic that she was casting, and beneath her a form had begun to take shape.

It wasn't long until she sat upon a magical unicorn, its body slightly transparent and its horn glowing brightly.

"Now it starts," Esme said. "You shall sit like this." She perched herself on the crook between the unicorn's neck and its back. "And you shall not fall off. Now approach. If you are chosen, you will already know which unicorn belongs to you."

While the dragon-riding cats sat and watched, the unicorn-riding-cats-to-be let out a series of loud yowls – their war cry – and they charged forwards. They flowed around Esme, Bastet, and me like a river. The charge quickly split into rivulets that then in turn narrowed into smaller streams. Before I knew it cats were leaping into the air, jumping three times their height onto the backs of unicorns.

Some of the unicorns whinnied. Others reared with their forelegs in the air. As I had always said – horses cannot be trusted. I caught a glimpse of Bruno the massive Persian who looked as if he were about to get thrown off the side. But still, the cats managed to hold on. I have no idea how many claws were digging into the unicorns' hides to help the cats keep purchase. I guess it would be hurting the unicorns more than it had hurt the dragons.

"Now," Esme said. "Time for our first ride."

She turned her enchanted unicorn around and charged towards the paddock. At first I thought her mount would lower its horn and try to butt the others out of the way, but instead the unicorns parted quickly and naturally, allowing Esme room to surge through.

The Abyssinian threw her head upwards and tossed her staff into the sky. It didn't fall, but instead reached a steady level where it stayed as it cut through the air in the wake of Esme and her unicorn.

The unicorns in the magical paddock already had turned their heads towards Esme to watch her riding off into the distance.

They let out a collective neigh, which again didn't translate to mean anything in their telepathic language. Then they charged as a whole unit, kicking up clods of pink glowing dirt and grass.

Admittedly, I'd expected to see at least one cat fall off a unicorn. After experiencing how bad the dragon riding cats had been during their training at Bestian Academy, I didn't expect any better of these street cats. But they all held fast to their mounts, their bodies swaying from side to side in the opposite direction to the flow of their unicorns' bodies.

They were naturals. I guess they believed in their abilities and they also believed in Esme. I mean, who didn't?

"Now, it is time for Dragoncat to complete his first task," Bastet said. "Take it from here, please."

I turned back to the dragon riding cats. They seemed to have lost their insolence since our fight with the griffin; there was no moaning about the temperature, or how poor breakfast had been this morning, or the fact that they would rather go back to sleep. They weren't even grooming themselves or lying down and curling up into a ball or finding any other way to not pay attention. Instead, they seemed eager to learn.

"I'm afraid the first task won't be easy," I said, "because we need to wake our dragons, and we need to do it now!"

That caused all the cats to groan and growl a little. Everyone knew that dragons didn't like to be awoken. When they got angry, they tended to breathe fire. Salanraja would take some flak from the other dragons for it, of course, given it was me that had given the order. So I expected her to be the most angry of them all.

But now the cats were obedient, and together we called out to our dragons by screaming in our minds. It wasn't long until the horizon responded with a collective and incredibly loud roar.

Shortly after, two hundred angry dragons approached from the direction of Bastet's lair and we all feared their wrath.

27

HOW TO BECOME POWERFUL

In truth, there wasn't really any reason for us to be scared of our dragons. It was all in our minds.

Dragons are notoriously quick to anger but they're also quick to forgive, at least the creature that they are bonded to. So though Salanraja moaned at me during the flight over to us about how I had not only rudely awakened her but also ordered all the cats to awaken their dragons, she neglected to act on her threat to pass a few flames over my fur before landing.

"*Bastet told me to do it,*" I pleaded, in an attempt to placate her mood. I felt it inside my chest when she was angry as well, and I really didn't like that feeling.

"*That's no excuse,*" Salanraja replied inside my mind. "*You can't blame a goddess for your actions.*"

"*But she said it was destiny. I didn't have any choice.*"

"*And now that's even worse. Instead of blaming a goddess you're choosing to blame an abstract concept instead.*"

"*I thought you were saying that this destiny stuff wasn't nonsense?*"

"*I did,*" Salanraja said. "*But that doesn't mean it's not abstract.*"

"*What's the difference?*" I asked.

"*Never mind. I wouldn't expect a lesser mind like yours to understand.*"

I ignored her insult – I just wasn't in the mood for Salanraja's nonsense.

I didn't just hear the heavy rhythm of beating wings approaching, but I could smell the sulphur on the dragons' breath.

To make her point, Salanraja hit the ground with a huge thud that caused it to shudder for a moment, made even worse when all the dwarf dragons landed in exactly the same fashion. The dragons formed a wide circle around me, Bastet and our army of around two hundred cats.

It was on that note that our training for the day began.

I didn't need to teach the cats how to fly; they knew that already. But I needed to teach them how to cast magic. So first I had them mount their dragons, then I instructed them to summon their staff bearers.

All of the cats looked to me, with their staffs in their mouths, the crystals on them glowing all kinds of different colours. The dragons that they were standing on seemed more impatient than the cats this time. Salanraja had told me that none of them understood why they had to be there if I was teaching the cats magic, but I assured her it was all part of the plan.

Thus, from my position on Salanraja's head, raised up even higher than Bastet stood, I addressed my students. As I spoke the wind picked up to amplify my voice, which I now realised was part of Bastet's magic.

"I think I know what the problem has been," I said. "Why you've not been able to find your magic, and it hasn't been a matter of time. Bastet has helped me understand."

There came a murmuring of meows from the cats, and for a

moment I thought I might have lost them. But I only let my words hang in the air for a moment, before I continued to speak and the wind continued to augment my voice.

"It comes down to how you feel inside. How much you believe in yourself, and how much you believe in your bond with your dragon." At those words, the dragons seemed to perk up a little. I had clearly struck a chord. "You stand here on the plains above the River of Souls, and your very life force dances and pulses beneath you. But have you noticed that some containers have two souls?"

The cats let out some chirps of agreement. Clearly, they'd been much more observant than I'd thought. I turned to Bastet. I thought it better that she explained this part, so it sounded all mystical and ethereal. Her voice trilled with that soft Welsh lilt as she spoke, although I'm sure every cat here heard her differently.

"When you bonded with your dragon," Bastet said. "The lanterns holding your souls merged together in this realm and you became a collective whole. That is why it's so devastating for a dragon to lose their rider or a rider to lose their dragon. The absence is felt in this dimension, as a single soul tries to find meaning in a vessel meant for two."

"And it is just the same for magic. In order to use it most effectively, you need to accept the bonding of your own soul with your dragon's. Mould yourself into shape as you draw upon not only your own power, but the power that is formed through your bond. If you do this, your magic will become strong, and you will be a force to be reckoned with. Learn not to act alone, but together with your dragons and your comrades whom you fought beside, and then the warlocks won't know what hit them."

The cats lined up before us let out a sequence of appreciative chirps and meows. Bastet now had lit the flame that would inspire hope in my students, and she looked down at me clearly expecting me to fuel it.

"Mounted on your dragons," I said, "you shall learn together how it's done. As you fly, remember your bond with your dragons and remember that we are all part of a team." I looked at Rex, who lifted his tail and blinked slowly. "Now, together let's discover how it's done."

Without even waiting for a response, from my position on Salanraja's head, I summoned my staff bearer to place my staff in my mouth.

"*I hope you realise, Bengie,*" Salanraja said as we took off, "*that after the brutal manner in which you awoke me this morning, I'm not going to make this flight easy on your stomach.*"

"*Just don't do anything to show me up,*" I said. "*Please . . . this is important. The fate of the worlds depends on it.*"

"*Fine,*" Salanraja said. "*But every single dwarf dragon flying behind us wants to hear you personally apologise to them later.*"

"*The things I do in the name of destiny,*" I said.

"*What?*"

"*Nothing,*" I said, and I turned over my shoulder to see the neat box-formation of dwarf dragons that flew behind us. The cats upon their heads looked awfully confident, and within their mouths they clasped staffs with coloured crystals on the ends, glowing bright with nascent magic.

They were changing – I could see that. And I was starting to believe we actually might have a chance.

28

TRAINING TIME

Naturally, the cat students – both those who rode unicorns and those who rode dragons – didn't learn the ways of magic in a single day. It takes time for these things to soak in, and the feline brain admittedly hasn't been designed for such stuff. We're intrinsically wired to hunt, not to manipulate matter with our minds or engage warlocks and their minions in mortal combat.

Still, our first training session in the Fifth Dimension went a lot better than I'd expected. Bastet provided glamours of spectral manipulators and their rake-ribbed bone dragons that the cats and their dragons would one day have to fight for real. Suffice it to say that the magic which emerged from the dragon riding cats' staffs didn't just fizzle and pop this time. Rather, it came out in untrained beams of fire, ice, lightning, and nature. Ta'ra brought down several manipulators all by herself, and a good number of the cats managed to also bring down one or two. All the while, the dragons battled against the bone dragons in the sky, bringing them down with exemplary performance, as they always had.

Still, Bastet's magical simulation overwhelmed them, leaving the whole terrain stinking of rotten vegetable juice for a moment until she had magicked it all away. Clearly, much more work needed to be done.

We slept and we ate, and we trained some more, and within a few days around half of our number had become quite accomplished. There were around two hundred dragon riders amongst my students. The simulated manipulators on the ground cast up an army of bone dragons with their spectral beams, and so the dragons deposited the cats on the ground.

I watched from Salanraja's back in the sky as the cats surged forward as a unit, the shield mage cats casting protective domes over their allotted squadrons. These shields flickered out at calculated intervals to allow the other cat mages to cast forth their magic.

Meanwhile, fire scorched the earth; ice ran in fast moving bolts over the ground; vines twisted and wrapped around the spectral staffs of the manipulators, wrenching them out of their grasps; lightning flashed from enemy to enemy. The whole scene was a spectacle of lights and chaos.

The manipulators fought back, but they couldn't hit a single cat. None of the feline shield mages were as precise and as brave as Lars had been – in fact, some of the manipulators' magic did break through an occasional shield. But the cats had the benefit of being smaller than humans, which made them harder to hit.

It wasn't long until the battle was over, and my heart leaped with joy when I realised how little time had passed. My students had defeated an army of manipulators in the space of around fifteen minutes. Our fabled feline dragon riders were becoming a formidable force.

As I continued to train the dragon riding cats, Esme trained the unicorn riding ones, and Aleam took some time to teach Rine,

Ange, Bellari, Asinda, and Seramina some new skills. We didn't have Matharon here to train the dragons, but we did have the mighty dragons Corralsa and Olan, who were considered seniors. So they took all the dragons on practise flights, although Salanraja told me multiple times that these weren't as gruelling as Matharon's had been. But I guess that was a good thing; we didn't want to enter battle against the warlocks with exhausted dragons.

The Sussex spaniel, Max, on the other hand would be quite selective about who he wanted to train with. Sometimes he'd come flying with us and helping to fight the manipulators, but other days he'd be surfing on his magical board along with the unicorns. Apparently he liked to fly rings around them and scream at them that they needed to battle the wargs. It was almost as if he believed them sheep and himself a sheepdog with a super powered board instead of legs. I can imagine that it quite annoyed the unicorns. Even today it makes me chuckle inside whenever I envision it.

Max would join Aleam's lessons on other days, and sometimes he'd just go wandering off across the realm by himself, his nose pressed closed to the ground, sniffing after who knows what. A trail of wargs, no doubt; Max always seemed to be on the lookout for wargs.

I worried often, as did many of the other cats, that we would run out of time. According to Bastet, the First Dimension had only a few days before Alliander and the warlocks would summon Ammit out of the Seventh Dimension. Then it would take them about an hour, assuming they had placed the Grand Crystal correctly, to complete the maleficent spell that would break the worlds. If that happened we'd know immediately, because demons would be able to swarm into every dimension including the Fifth, taking it over within seconds.

Bastet's mortal enemy, the demon snake Apopis, had apparently made quite a recovery in the Seventh Dimension since he'd retreated back into it to recover. He'd no doubt hunt her down, with an army of demon animals. In short we'd be doomed.

But Bastet reassured us that time passed differently in the Fifth Dimension. It was all relative really as to how the souls perceived time. A single hour could seem like an eternity for a soul, or it could flash by like a brief second. To put it more simply, if we believed that we had time to spare, then we did. But once that belief started to dwindle, then it would be time to go to battle, and I had learned enough of our destinies to understand that there would be no turning back.

We were preparing for the final battle against the warlocks, the demons of the Seventh Dimension, and the dark force *Cana Dei*, which had terrorised us for so long.

In short, either we won or everything died.

29

RESTING TIME

When I'd said that there was no way to know when day passed into night in the Fifth Dimension, I hadn't told the whole truth. We did have Bastet, and she could sense the flow of time not just in this dimension, but across all of them. Thus it was down to her to tell us when it was time to train and when it was time to rest.

Naturally, the harder we trained the harder we rested. So I would spend a long time sleeping during those rest sessions, and I spent a little less time, not that it was any less important, grooming myself alongside my *companion*, Ta'ra.

Sometimes during these rest sessions, we cats would visit the humans in the hut and curl up on one of their laps in the living room area. If all the laps were taken, the warm fireplace was also a popular choice. The hearth provided ample heat to the room, and gave the whole place a sweet scent of wood-smoke. Just like outside, nothing in this room was coloured like it would normally be in the real world. Everything had pink outlines instead, with black spaces in between. When something was constantly in motion, like the flames of the fire, the pink seemed to dance around the dark patches in a hypnotic display. It made me go cross-eyed just watching it.

Rine, Ange, Seramina, Aleam, Bellari, Max and a selection of regular cats including me, Ta'ra, Esme, Geni, and Bruno – not to mention Ange's desert cheetah Palimali – frequented the living room most often. But I don't think I ever saw Asinda in there.

Her grief caused her to keep mostly to herself, and I was still avoiding her. It wasn't that I didn't like her, but I still didn't know how to handle her, and after what I'd done I feared she might attack me on sight.

I'd often hear her weeping in her room upstairs and I knew that Ta'ra, Esme and Max would creep in to comfort her. Ta'ra and Esme could both speak the human language, and Max could also but he refused to speak anything but dog. Still, none of them told me what they talked about to Asinda, and after Aleam had told me off for eavesdropping I didn't want to try and find out. Truth be told, I already felt guilty about forcing Asinda into this dimension and I didn't want to make that guilt even worse.

One day, I was hunting a magical butterfly all the way over to the River of Souls when I saw Asinda sitting staring down at the water. She had placed herself awfully close to the edge of the canyon and, from what I understood of the River of Souls, if she fell in there would be no coming back.

The reflections of the canyon walls and the inlaid lanterns with their pink lights inside them glimmered over the dark water, which roared along its path towards the void at the end of it all.

The butterfly I'd been chasing floated right over Asinda's head and did a circle in front of her. As it did so, it caught her eye. I turned to leave her be, but as if tempting fate, the butterfly did a one eighty and went fluttering back towards me.

Of course, no cat ignores a butterfly when it comes within

swiping range. I raised myself on my hind legs in an attempt to catch it in my paws, but the butterfly was too high. Then I heard Asinda call out to me. She was glaring at me in the scary way that she used to when she'd first met me.

"Ben!"

"Asinda," I said. "You shouldn't get too close to the water, you know. If you fall in, then . . ."

She shook her head without breaking that harsh glare. "I can do what I like, as we've already established. I have free will, don't I?"

I considered telling her how we needed her alive, so she could play her destined part in the fight against the warlocks. But I decided that would perhaps be a little too heavy handed. It would also give her extra fodder for an argument that I sensed she was gearing herself up for. So instead I just stood and stared back at her, my tail thrashing against the ground and my ears twitching.

"Just come over here a moment, Ben," Asinda said. "I'd rather talk than shout."

I figured I had no better choice. I stalked over to her cautiously. Instinct was telling me that she might even try to throw me into the river. *No, she wouldn't do that, surely?*

"Would you at least step back from the edge?" I asked as I approached.

"But I like it here," Asinda said, as she kicked her legs against the wall of the canyon. "The way the breeze brushes against my cheeks. The freshness of the air coming from the water. It reminds me how I used to be when I was younger. Free to run around the playgrounds. Free to do whatever I pleased. I wish . . ." She trailed off, as if her thought had become lost in the void.

Silence hung in the air for a moment, disturbed only by the whistling of the breeze. Beneath us, the froth on the water glowed pink. In their containers on the opposite wall, the souls seemed to shiver, as if acknowledging Asinda's grief. I could smell the stress seeping out of her pores, and I could tell how she just wanted to let go. But still I could see the fire in her eyes that told her she had to hold on, that she needed to be there to see the last battle through, at least so that Lars wouldn't have sacrificed himself in vain.

"Look, I'm sorry," I said, after letting the silence hang for a moment. I figured those were the words she wanted to hear.

Asinda gave me a curious frown. "For what, exactly?"

"I'm sorry that I forced you into this dimension. I'm sorry I separated you from—"

Asinda raised her hand then quickly clicked her fingers, cutting me off. "I don't want to hear it, Ben. I don't want to relive it all over again. I just . . ."

She puffed out her cheeks, then exhaled through pursed lips. She wiped a tear from the corner of her eye with the back of her hand. The butterfly returned for another round, and I turned my head to watch it. But this time I didn't chase after it; it just didn't seem appropriate.

"You know what I learned just a few days before all this happened?" Asinda said. "The mother and father that I grew up with – they weren't really my mother and father. I had a couple of days' leave, and they came clean. My mother actually was the same I'd always thought she was, but do you know who my real father was?"

I didn't answer. I kind of sensed she didn't want me to, so I just waited for her to continue.

"It was Arran," Asinda said. "The Warlock Prince, who almost ended up destroying everything. Lasinta was his grandmother, and I am a part of their line. Of course, Arran never admitted to anyone he was my father. He was much too proud for that.

"But it means I'm a warlock's daughter as well, making me no different from Seramina. So why did she have to go through every-thing she did? Why didn't *Cana Dei* just pick me?"

"I don't know," I said, without even thinking about it. "Maybe it was scared of you."

When the crystals gifted me with the ability to speak all languages, they didn't teach me not to speak before I had time to first think about what I was saying. I just couldn't stop the words tumbling out of my mouth.

Asinda's face went red. "What did you say?"

"I mean—"

Asinda's eyes had closed to narrowed slits now, she clenched her fists and I readied myself to flee. I watched her eyes, and I watched her hands, expecting her to draw her staff and hit me some of that warlock's-daughter magic.

Instead she snorted, and then she was cackling out loud, unable to contain her laughter. The emotions surged out of her, and the mirth soon turned to tears.

Now cats generally don't like being near humans when they're in hysterics. It scares us and it's too loud for us to cope with. So instinctively my legs urged me to run away, but at the same time I sensed Asinda needed me to be here.

The young woman composed herself and took a few deep breaths. Then, apart from her red-rimmed eyes, she looked as if she hadn't expressed any emotions at all.

"I know what you meant," she said, rubbing her eyes. "You find me scary like everyone always used to. I'd always been like that, until I met Lars. He taught me how to get on with people. He taught me how to smile, and how to wear my hair right, and how to be respected by others. He changed me in so many ways I can't express. He loved me . . . and I loved him so much."

"I didn't mean to say that you were scary," I said. "It just came out wrong."

"It doesn't matter now," Asinda said, shaking her head. "Lars, and my love for him, kept *Cana Dei* from me, and now he's gone. I don't have him to protect me anymore. Maybe now *Cana Dei* will take the opportunity to close in, and claim me like you say it claimed Alliander."

"No it won't," I said.

"And how do you know that?"

"Because you know who you are. You are one of the strongest people I know . . ."

Asinda took another deep breath. She stood up and stepped back from the edge. Then she examined the crystals along the length of it. For a moment they glowed purple, and I caught a whiff of rotten vegetable juice. Fire flashed at the back of Asinda's eyes.

Then it was all gone, and Asinda was looking out at the wall of souls across the river, composing herself. "Thank you Ben," she said. "You're a good friend."

"Don't mention it," I answered, and as we walked back together to the camp, I remembered what Aleam had told me about inspiring hope in others. He was right, it was easy. Once I had hope myself, then I would be able to give hope to others too.

It was at that moment that a strange thought came to my head. What if Alliander and the warlocks could be saved? What if none of us had to die and I could just banish *Cana Dei* from their minds? But I had no idea how I would even begin to do that. And so I pushed the thought away, guiltily hoping it would never come to me again.

30

INTRODUCING GOLEMS

The next day, Bastet decided to ramp up the training, and she did so by introducing golems into the mix.

Fire golems, clay golems, forest golems, stone golems. Each of them was a formidable foe in its own right, and of course I feared the worst for my feline dragon rider students. I just couldn't rid myself of the concern that we were training them too fast and that we would send them into battle against the warlocks far too soon.

But then, what choice did we have?

Again, I watched from on high, this time not on Salanraja's back but near the edge of a clifftop. Salanraja stood on my right, her head cocked with interest. She had taken some time off from flight training with Corralsa and Olan so she could help me provide instruction if necessary.

Bastet stood on my left, with her forepaws curled around the rim of the cliff. She had her eyes shut and remained completely still as she cast the glamour of the simulation that the cats would face today. This time, she had conjured it to look exactly like the Darklands, with purple smelly mist seeping up from cracks in the ground. The only signs of life were the dead husks of trees that had lived in this land before it became scorched and ruined by dark magic, and a tall field of purple glowing mushrooms, their heads looming taller than the height of two tall men stacked one atop the other.

The dragon riding cats waited in a barren valley with their staffs in their mouths, clearly visible against the grey and colourless earth. They looked up towards a dark hill with only a few mounds of separated boulders as its most prominent feature. The mushrooms stood between them and their simulated enemies, their stalks a natural obstruction which the cats would have to deal with while casting their magic. Glowing purple spores filled the air around the mushrooms, looking as ominous as if they might poison any creature who breathed them in.

Bastet was to summon the golems on top of a steep a hill that rose sharply above the landscape, a crater dug into its top. In the centre of the crater loomed the Warlocks' Tower, one mighty cylinder leading the eye up towards the seven-spoked stone platform that hovered above it, rotating slowly around its axis. Bastet had even added the Grand Crystal in the centre of the platform to remind us of what we faced. It sent out a purple light from its facets and waves of smelly purple mist billowing outwards as it cast its magic over the land.

The dark hill the tower stood upon presented a sharp contrast to the vibrant purple mushrooms that surrounded it. They had apparently only appeared there very recently, created through the powerful magic of the Grand Crystal. No normal creature could charge through that forest unaided by magic – the spores would suffocate them before they reached the other side.

Bees buzzed in front of the cats. Dragonflies and butterflies graced the air around them. I had asked Bastet to put them in, because I'd already given the cats a lecture about not letting anything distract them.

Cana Dei was clever enough to be able to create a glamour of its own, and I could imagine it sending a swarm of butterflies to create turmoil in my students' ranks. If they relied on instinct alone, they'd be dropping their staffs and chasing the butterflies, and so I wanted to guard against this potential scenario. In all honesty, I'd seen a foretelling of this exact scene in the crystals back at the Versta Caverns.

I saw the heads of a few cats, including Rex, follow the butterflies as they flew by. As we'd agreed, Salanraja let out a loud roar from beside me to remind them to pay attention. Then Bastet cast the glamour, and the battle started.

The fire golems appeared on the hill first, starting as sparks of amber light and soon becoming floating flames. Within moments, they gathered energy and launched themselves off the ground, a group of flying bombs heading for the army of cats.

There came a series of yowls from the ranks below. Cats communicate as a flock, like crows keeping watch and warning others of any danger. White light flashed from the shield mages' staffs, and they cast out domes of magical kinetic energy. They seemed somehow stronger than they had been a week ago, the shields wavering less and the flickering less intermittent. We'd need that when we faced off against real fire golems. Any unnecessary breaks and heat could fill the shield, frying the cats inside.

The fire golems blazed through the sky like flaming cannonballs. These magical creatures were easily killed, as their magical life was snuffed out as soon as they exploded. Yet this created much carnage, arguably making them the most dangerous of all the golems.

The magical projectiles hit the shields and burst into flame, and even from up here I felt the heat that Bastet had added to the scenario. The fire washed over the lattice of shields that the cats had created, but none of them managed to penetrate the barriers. The cats had survived the first wave.

Next came the clay golems. These magical creations were a vexation to shield mages, since they could get right underneath anything, including magical barriers. Clay golems moved by temporarily turning the rock beneath their feet to clay, which then became part of their form. They were thus constantly morphing while in motion, never having a defined shape. The only way to defeat them was through knocking out both of their crystal eyes, one red and one blue.

A troop of twenty clay golems seeped down from the hill, keeping close to the ground as the low purple mist concealed them from view. They were hard to see, and the cats would have a difficult time tracking them. The milky wall of the shield barrier would certainly make them harder to detect, and so the feline shield mages stepped back, including Geni.

I wasn't focused on her but instead on the ten feline leaf mages, whom I had trained to fight these creatures. They stalked forwards, the green crystals on their staffs glowing brightly. For a moment they watched, crouched against the ground, as the golems slithered and snaked through the mushroom forest.

Then there came a great roar from in front of them, and the clay golems leaped out of their hiding places. Three of them had found their way to a spot right in front of the cats, and others slid in quickly from the sides, trying to flank them.

For a moment I thought they were going to take the cats unaware. But now the feline mages had the instinct trained into them to cast their magic. Out of their staffs came a network of vines and branches, whipping out at the faces of the clay golems. Within moments the crystals were wrenched out of their sockets, and the golems melted back into the earth.

That was round two done and dusted, and now a third wave of golems came in, this time forest golems. These started out as whirlwinds around a central core. Their pull was so strong that they sucked out forest matter from all around them. As they tore through the mushroom woodland, they shredded pieces off the massive funguses, adding substance to their form.

Soon enough, sufficient matter surrounded the crystals at the heart of the golems, so that it could compact into much more solid material. The whirlwinds were now great looming towers, spinning forward, ready to knock down anything that got in their way. Massive arms with solid fists had formed out of their substance, and it seemed they had enough power in them to knock dragons out of the sky.

The leaf mages fell back and the fire mages stepped forwards, the staff in each cat's mouth having a red glowing crystal at the tip. The forest golems continued to lumber forward, and the fire mages didn't have much time. They worked as one, sending out strong jets of blue fire which quickly extended into streams of amber flame. The torrents washed forwards, as the forest golems continued to dredge through the blaze.

For a moment, it looked as if they would break through. Yet the cats continued to generate fire and their flames grew even brighter. The forest golems reached the cats and I saw massive fists rise into the sky, ready to crush anything beneath them. But at the same time, the rest of their bodies were already blackening, and one by one the golems erupted into flame.

The golems shrunk into blackened shreds that quickly became ash. The crystals that had been at their core glowed red for a moment and then they too fell to the floor, both the magic and momentum drained out of them.

The cats had survived a third round, yet it still wasn't over. Now the came the grandest golems of them all – stone golems, two of them, sheer giant lumps of moving humanoid rock with crystals hidden deep within. They quaked the ground as they moved, easily three times the height of Bastet, with limbs that could knock down walls and crush towers. Indeed, they were formidable foes, and hence required powerful magic to conjure.

The golems approached one after the other, slowly but surely across the blackened ground that previously had contained mushrooms and spores. They lined up, one in front and the other behind, where it would be shielded from the cats' spells.

This time, the ice mages stepped forwards with blue crystals on their staffs. Out of them they cast solid jets of ice at the first stone golem, but that did nothing except create a patch of blue on its chest. The two stone golems continued to lumber forwards. The cats had less than a minute before they crushed them all.

But the feline ice mages didn't give up, just as I had taught them. They continued to cast ice at the same point of the stone golem's chest, and the blue cold point extended outwards. Slowly, a layer of frost and rime spanned across the stone golem's surface. This solidified into icicles and then glaciers that swelled out from the golem, halting it in place.

Some of the ice mages below shuffled to the side to let the few lightning mages forward. Their staffs had yellow crystals, and they were already summoning energy from the sky. They threw out several balls of bolt lightning that converged on the frozen golem. Once they hit, they sparked and fizzled and then out erupted a sequence of incredibly loud bangs, providing enough force to shatter stone. The ice crumbled, and then it thawed under the intense heat of the lightning. The stone golem crumbled to a pile of rubble, and from that it didn't rise.

Still, there was one stone golem left, and it clambered over its fallen colleague, gaining speed. I could see how the cats had now expended all their energy. They didn't have anything left to defeat this one.

Except there was one cat who hadn't played her part yet – my good *companion*, Ta'ra stepped forwards, the fairy dust that made up her golden staff glistening brightly. She held this in her mouth and she cast out a bolt of energy, so soft it almost seemed to whisper.

The stone golem looked down at her with red menacing eyes, and it quickly clutched its hands together and rolled its fists around in a haymaker that looked like it would bat the Cat Sidhe from one side of the Fifth Dimension to the other.

At the same time, Ta'ra's staff bearer winked into existence just beside her. It swept downwards to yank the staff out of Ta'ra's mouth, leaving her enough space to scream the word, "*Butterflies!*" at the top of her lungs.

It wasn't a lump of stone that assaulted her, but a flock of the very creature she had just named. I heard her cry out in delight, then reach up to try and catch a butterfly in her paws. The rest of the flock continued past her, right into the clowder behind. Now that the cats had realised the battle was over, they also decided it was the perfect opportunity to dart around trying to catch the butterflies that Ta'ra had magicked out of thin air.

31

ONE FINAL EXERCISE

Bastet opened her eyes and turned to me. A purr was coming from deep in her throat, the vibrations so powerful that they also rumbled through the rock beneath us so that I felt them in my paws.

Below us, in the valley filled with cats, the glamour disappeared. They found themselves no longer in a simulation of the Darklands beneath the Warlocks' tower, but in the Fifth Dimension surrounded by the pink glowing edges that defined everything in this realm.

"It is good," Bastet said. "I think you are ready."

A growl came unbidden from my throat. "How can we be ready?" I asked. "None of the cats have faced warlocks or wisp dragons, and there are so many more scenarios they might encounter."

"We have not got time to cover everything," Bastet said. "And this is enough."

"But you said that we had plenty of time, as long as you believed."

"And yet your faith is dwindling," she answered. "I can feel it in the ebb and flow of time. Not just that, but your students are eager to test their power. Hold them here too long and they will once again start to doubt their worth."

I padded at the ground with my paws, and I checked myself. It wasn't long until I realised that my fear wasn't regarding my concern for my students but about me.

I was naturally a cat, and a huge part of me didn't want to go into battle. But I'd learned during my time with the humans that I needed to make sacrifices for the greater good, as did we all.

A surge of pride welled up in my chest as I considered this. Humans had survived so long because they knew how to work together, and now these cats had learned to work not just with their own dragons but as a part of a collective team of fellow felines as well.

"Does this mean the battle will commence?" I asked.

"It does . . ."

"Tonight?" I asked.

"No," Bastet said. "You have one more night to rest. This is how fate has willed it, and this is how it's going to be. But you must go in strong, so there is time for one final feast."

Her golden eyes seemed to glisten for a moment as her words hung in the air. Then, without a pause, she pulled herself back onto her haunches and sailed through the air towards the valley floor below. My stomach lurched as I watched her do it, and for a moment I forgot that she was an immortal goddess, almost as old as time itself.

Time seemed to slow as she dived through the darkness, and as soon as she landed she was immediately striding over the valley floor, sprinting back towards her lair. I'd never seen a cat move with more grace, not even Esme.

The cats in the valley stopped chasing the butterflies that Ta'ra had summoned and watched her. It only took them a moment to decide that they all wanted to abandon their play and instead chase after Bastet. I guessed she'd told them inside their minds about the imminent feast.

I considered the cliff edge, peering down into the darkness.

"*Don't even think about following her, Bengie,*" Salanraja said from beside me.

I looked up at her yellow eyes high above me. "*I was just considering whether I could climb down. Maybe there's enough ledges.*"

"*Or you could just jump on my back, and we could get off this cliff the easy way. If you're fast enough, we'll probably beat the other cats for the first bite of hot smoked salmon.*"

I meowed as she said those final words. "*What did you say?*"

"*Hot smoked salmon,*" Salanraja said again. "*Bastet thinks there's no better food to make the cats strong.*"

"*Are you teasing me, Salanraja?*"

"*No,*" she replied. "*You have my word.*"

And her word was enough to get my mouth salivating. I immediately scurried up her back, taking my place at the crook of her neck.

"*Hurry up, then,*" I said. "*I don't want to arrive and find there's nothing left.*"

"*Affirmative, sir,*" Salanraja replied, and she took off into the air.

32

ONE FINAL FEAST

Alas, Salanraja didn't fly gently and evenly on the way back to Bastet's lair. Instead she decided to execute a complex series of dives, barrel rolls and loop the loops. I tried not to complain, because I knew doing so would be likely to cause her to fly even more erratically.

She was taking liberties, of course. She knew that I wanted her to keep her promise that I'd be first amongst the cats to get the smoked salmon – I did deserve it after all. She proceeded to fly just the way she wanted to on the way there, knowing she had the upper claw.

I worried that I might arrive with such an unsettled stomach that I wouldn't even want my favourite food. I'd only eaten smoked salmon once since I'd been yanked away from my home in the Fourth Dimension, and I'd longed for it ever since.

But as my dragon had promised, we did arrive ahead of the other cats, but not in front of Bastet, who had already summoned a familiar glamour outside her lair. From above, the pink and black earth shifted suddenly to a loamy forest floor surrounded by pine trees huddled together at its edges like gathered soldiers. The way the darkness led into the glamour made it look like some kind of island in the centre of a sea of oil.

A clearing spanned the centre of the forest. It was large enough to host the mighty Bastet herself, all the dragons who had already landed, the street cats of Cimlean City and their unicorns, Max and the several humans among our number, and, once they arrived, the dragon riding cats.

All but my own students had gathered around a roaring campfire, with spits speared through massive fish revolving over it. Often during such traditional feasts, the food had been turned by a turnspit wheel that Max had loved to run on – since for some reason dogs seemed to believe in working for their food. But there was no sign of any such device, and so I presumed it was all worked instead by Bastet's magic.

I caught a whiff of woodsmoke, and then an even stronger aroma of the salmon juices. My tummy was rumbling so loudly, and I needed to be down on the ground quickly.

Already, Max, the unicorns, and the cats had bowls of fish in front of them, and all three types of creatures were lapping it up hungrily. There were enough bowls free for the other cats when they arrived, and presumably for me as well. But I wanted the salmon straight from the source.

As if she understood my urgency, Salanraja slammed herself down next to the fire, sending up a flurry of dry leaves. Even before her tail touched the ground, I was running down it, the scent of smoked fish filling my lungs. Aleam and Rine stood near the food, carving pieces of the pink flesh off onto a large fork.

Rine saw me and dangled a strip of salmon over me, low enough to be just within reach. I raised myself on my hind paws and tried to claim the salmon with my mouth, but Rine raised the fork.

"Put that salmon down immediately," I demanded. "It doesn't belong on that fork. It belongs in my stomach."

"I *could*," Rine said. "But just do that begging thing you did again. It was kind of cute."

"I wasn't begging. I was trying to get the food."

"Okay, so one more time," Rine said, a smirk on his hard-boned face that I wanted to slash off with a claw. "Stand on your hind legs and pretend you're a dog." He lowered the fork once more, and I watched his eyes, knowing that if I went for the food, he'd only raise the fork again.

"Oh just give the cat the food already," Bellari shouted.

"Yeah," Ange said. "You can be such a big meanie sometimes, Rine."

The two girls sat next to each other on a log. Ange had a plate in her lap and she was picking her way through her meal with her fingers. Bellari didn't have one, so I assumed she'd already eaten.

"You heard them," I said. "You don't want to make your *girl-friends* angry."

Rine's eyebrows lowered into a frown, then he shrugged and dropped the salmon to the ground. I dove on it immediately, tearing pieces off the thick bones. Much of this scene was clearly a glamour, but the fish and the fire were real, and it was the best smoked salmon I'd ever tasted. I let the juices roll over my tongue as I heard footsteps padding over to me.

Ta'ra stepped into view, and I glared at it her in warning not to dare touch my food, before diving in for another mouthful.

"I wouldn't disturb him," Rine warned. "Nothing can stand between Ben and his hot smoked fish, not even his first love."

"Stay out of it," I grumbled without even looking up. I kept my words short though; I was too busy enjoying the food.

It must have been good five minutes later that I found myself licking my lips and looking up to see who was near me. Bellari and

Ange sat in the same place. Ange was still picking at her food, slowly chewing, clearly engaging in that weird human activity that they call 'savouring it'.

I leaped up between the two girls. To my surprise, Bellari reached out to stroke me first. I curled up next to her, then my tail raised up in alarm when I realised that I didn't smell fish on her breath but instead yucky courgettes.

"You didn't have any salmon?" I asked her.

"No," Bellari said, shaking her head. Her cheeks had gone slightly red. "I'm allergic."

"What, to salmon? You've never eaten it before."

"To all fish," Bellari said. "To seafood in fact. I'm allergic to a lot of things."

"Are you sure it's not psychosomatic?"

"Psycho—" Bellari rolled the syllables around on her tongue as if testing them. "Oh, that word again. Why do you have to bring up the strange magic that they use in the Fourth Dimension again?"

"It's not magic, it's science."

"Same thing . . ."

"It really isn't," I said, licking my lips for a second time.

It was then that I noticed that Bellari seemed a little distant about something. I figured that it was something to do with the conversation before, but I didn't feel it necessary to quiz her about it. Instead, I tucked my head into her lap, and rested it there a moment so my purrs could provide her some comfort. Ange stroked my tail which caused me to purr even more.

I didn't stay there forever, though. Instead, I caught sight of Asinda and Seramina sitting on separate logs on the other side of the fire. They seemed to be sharing a moment, but at the same time they weren't talking to each other. Instead they just stared into the flames, the plates of food hardly touched on their laps.

I decided that if they weren't going to eat any of their meal, then I was quite welcome to help myself to some. I mean it was smoked salmon after all. But Ta'ra and Esme were already curled up on either side of Asinda, and other cats had found places at her feet.

It was clear the red-haired young woman didn't need any more company, so I sauntered over to Seramina instead. She didn't glance at me as I leaped up next to her, so I went up to her plate and took a bite of her food.

"It's delicious," I said, licking my lips. "Why haven't you touched any?"

"Huh?" Seramina's gaze drifted over to me slowly, then she looked down at her plate. She didn't seem to mind that I'd stolen some. "Oh, that. I'm just not so keen I guess." She shrugged. "I mean, it's okay. But it's not mutton sausages."

"Of course it's not," I said. "It's the most delicious food in all the dimensions." I took another bite.

"Each to their own, I guess." Seramina's gaze drifted back towards the fire.

How she couldn't like this stuff, I had no idea. Bastet had cooked it perfectly, and Bellari and Seramina really didn't know what they were missing.

"Hey, what's the matter?" I asked Seramina.

"What?"

"I said, what's the matter? You've lost your spirit, and you're meant to be the one who casts the final spell and saves us all."

Seramina sighed, turned her head away from the fire, but didn't look back down at me. Instead, her eyes focused on the darkness behind it all, or maybe her gaze simply became lost in there, just as she had twice almost lost herself to *Cana Dei*.

"You saw me in the Third Dimension, the Ghost Realm," she said. "But tell me again, what was I like?"

I edged closer to her, pushing up her hand which was clutching her plate in an attempt to get her to stroke me. She only raised her little finger in response, and so I rubbed my cheek against it.

"So?" she asked. "Tell me, Ben . . ."

"You were strong, Seramina," I said. "You were powerful, and I'm sure all the boys would have thought you a really beautiful woman."

"Is that right?" she asked, and I elicited none of the emotion I'd aimed for with my enthusiasm.

"Of course it is . . . Why wouldn't it be?"

Seramina broke off a piece of smoked salmon with her fork. She twizzled it around for a moment but didn't seem to want to lift it to her mouth to take a bite. Sensing this, I leaned forwards and snatched it right from her fork.

"Thank you," I said.

"You're welcome," Seramina replied.

"Now are you going to tell me what this is about?"

"It's just . . ." Seramina dropped her fork and put her hand on my neck. "I don't think I can do it, you know. All this time I've been raised knowing I was the daughter of perhaps the most powerful and singularly evil warlock who ever existed. Now, if I cast the spell that destroys the warlocks, what makes me any better than them?"

"But you know what will happen if we don't defeat them. They're not human, they've been taken over by *Cana Dei* . . ."

Seramina shook her head. "Ben, didn't you have the same dilemma when you faced off against me? You could have destroyed me and therefore stopped *Cana Dei* from using me to break the worlds. It's just got me thinking . . . What if we let the warlocks live? What if we can find another way?"

All of a sudden, the wind changed direction. It carried the

flames towards us for a second, bringing a pleasant heat and more of that delicious salmon scent. But then that faded, and I smelled something else behind it. It came from a distance, the stench of rotten vegetable juice. I squinted my eyes and saw purple flashes of lightning forming between the pink outlines of the clouds.

Every single living creature present turned their heads towards the sudden storm, even Bastet. And with it, as if Seramina's doubts had caused it, I felt hope evaporate from our camp.

The cats weren't happily munching on the smoked salmon anymore. I'd already detected Bellari's spirit starting to sink, but I also saw it in the slumped shoulders of Ange and Rine. Aleam was shaking his head and I heard a deep growl coming from Bastet, the one cat who never seemed to get angry.

Max whined and whimpered as he stared at the clouds, and I heard a murmur in the dog language, "Is that the wargs?"

I heard a shuffling of nearly a thousand paws behind me, and I glanced over my shoulder to see that the dragon riding cats had finally arrived, Ta'ra at their head. But they didn't have the same energy as they entered the clearing as they'd had after their simulated battle against the golems.

I turned back to see that the purple mist had started to roll in from the horizon, glowing as it came. My heart started to pound in my ribcage and more fearful thoughts assaulted my mind.

Because I had just realised that it had begun – the warlocks had started to channel the spell that would break the worlds.

33

THE PLAN UNVEILED

The storm raged in the distance, and though it hadn't reached us yet I could hear the rain pouring down. At the same time, my hackles had risen on the back of my neck, because Bastet had already told us that this wasn't normal rain. Instead, it was the kind that tears rifts in the fabric of space time, that reorders the universe as we know it. A torrent strong enough could open a portal to anywhere – enough of it and it would open a way for *Cana Dei* into this realm.

Bastet had ordered an emergency council for anyone designated a leader. The present party included me, Esme, Seramina, Asinda, Aleam, and – much to my surprise – Max. Two dragons were here too, Max's great jet-black dragon Corralsa, and Aleam's enormous white, Olan.

Out of all of us, I was the most vocal, but that was because I seemed the most scared. Cats like me just weren't built for thunderstorms, particularly ones that foretold the end of the worlds.

I just felt that my dragon riding cats weren't ready yet. And I didn't feel ready for that matter, either. Still, it was clear that the warlocks were breaking the worlds and so we didn't have another moment to train.

"We need to go now," I said. "Tonight . . . Otherwise all will be lost."

"Not now," Bastet said. "There is still time and if you enter the battle before your allies arrive, the warlocks will destroy you. You will have better strength in numbers."

Seramina, Asinda, and Aleam nodded their agreement. Esme looked at me with narrowed blue eyes, clearly wanting me to shut up. Max only whimpered; his ears were flattened against the sides of his head. Clearly he also didn't like the sound of the storm, though he seemed more agitated than scared.

"And what then?" I asked Bastet. "You want us to rest? Do you think any of us are going to get any sleep tonight?"

"If you don't sleep, at least you will have a chance to rest your muscles," Bastet said. "For all who trained today are tired."

I prepared myself to argue more, but Max's barking cut me off.

"Just shut up, Dragoncat," he said in the dog language. "Tomorrow we must be ready to fight all the wargs."

"They're not wargs, they're warlocks, and all of their magical creations."

"I told you before, I know what wargs are." He displayed his yellowed canine teeth with a growl and a snarl.

"Well, there probably will be wargs there," I said.

Max growled once again.

"He's right, you know," Esme said, and to my surprise she said it in the dog language. "There's nothing more we can do but wait."

"But you know how much I hate waiting," I said.

"Then just enjoy some time eating more smoked salmon."

"No . . ." Bastet said, back in the language that everyone could understand, spoken both out loud through magic and inside our own minds. "No more food for anyone. It's equally unwise to go into battle on a full stomach as on an empty one."

On that point, everyone seemed to agree except me. But who was I to argue? I only had to placate the dragon riding cats and give them enough hope that we could win so they had a chance of getting a good night's sleep.

Bastet continued to give us instructions. She told us of the enemies we might meet and gave us possible strategies for getting through the recently grown forest of giant mushrooms that now surrounded the Warlocks' Tower.

Our allies' job was to clear a path so that Bastet's Guardians of the White – namely Esme, Seramina, Asinda and I – could face off against the warlocks. By the time we arrived, Ammit would have already joined the warlocks, and together the seven of them would be channelling magic into the Grand Crystal. This would power the spell that would break the worlds.

Naturally, the only way up onto the stone platform that hovered above the Warlocks' Tower was to fly, and so we would need our dragons. So everyone else's job was to keep the ground clear of manipulators, which would help clear the sky of bone dragons and open up a path for us. No doubt the warlocks would have also cast other enemies such as ethereal wisp dragons. This was why we would need plenty of dragons and riders, as well as our White Mages on the ground.

The plan sounded so simple, and the way Bastet explained it I didn't see how we couldn't win. Once on the stone platform, we just needed to support Seramina, take down the warlocks, then together cast the spell that would break the Grand Crystal forever. *Cana Dei* at this point would be trapped in the crystal, and so by destroying it, we would destroy the dark force forever.

But as I looked up at Seramina I saw the same doubt in her

gaze that I'd noticed beside the campfire. The plan wouldn't work without her. Esme, Asinda, and I just weren't powerful enough to take down the warlocks and Ammit by ourselves.

Seramina caught me looking at her, and gave me a meek smile as if she knew exactly what I was thinking. In truth, I was worried that during our final battle against the warlocks, all because of Seramina's guilty conscience, she'd end up ruining it all.

34

IS IT LOVE?

Rather than sleeping with the other cats, I decided to spend the night in Seramina's bedroom. The silver-haired teenager clearly didn't like the look of the Fifth Dimension, and so instead she had cast a glamour spell to make her room look just like her one in Dragonsbond Academy. It had stone walls, a musty smell to it, a tallow candle on the trestle table opposite the door, and a coarse woollen blanket with that boring yet homely tan colour.

Ta'ra had agreed to accompany me tonight. My *companion* had told me that she wanted to spend this night close to my side. "Just in case," she'd said.

I'd already spoken with Rex, and he'd said that he'd give his dragon rider comrades a pep talk before they all slept, or would at least try to do so. He would be better at it than me, anyway. He had spent his life leading street cats over the rooftops of Cimlean City, then dropping down to scavenge food from the alleyways. Many nights, he'd told me, times had seemed so tough that he'd given plenty of speeches. Which is exactly what he planned to do this night.

I had hoped on the other hand to have a good talk with Seramina, to make sure that she wasn't going to back out and try to save the warlocks' lives. They'd kill us all before she had a chance to do so – they had lost their humanity long ago.

Alas, as soon as Seramina was under her blanket and her head hit the pillow, she was asleep. Soft snores were coming from her mouth, and I decided it probably wasn't a good idea to wake her. Maybe, after all, she'd feel a little better after a good night's rest. Seramina hadn't extinguished the candle, even though it was part of the glamour and she could probably do so with a click of her fingers. I guessed she was scared of the dark right now, with the storm and oblivion approaching and all. In truth, I think I was a little too.

Ta'ra and I curled up together at the foot of the bed, stretching out our forelegs to try and dominate as much room as possible. I could smell the smoked salmon on Ta'ra's breath, and I knew she'd had her fill of it. It made me proud that she was my *companion*, rather than Esme who had only apparently eaten a few mouthfuls.

The storm still raged outside, and I could sense it trying to roll closer. Bastet had cast some kind of magic to keep it out of her lair, and the river of souls also had some protective magic of its own that it drew from the Eighth Dimension – the void at the end of it all. But still I could hear the roars and crashes as the storm that was trying to tear apart space and time plugged at the protective barriers, trying its hardest to break through.

I turned my attention back to Ta'ra, who was lying in front of me. Since I'd known her, her face had lengthened, and her features had become even more feline. It was as if all the fairy that was left in her had seeped out, and now she only knew how to be a cat, and a spectacular one at that. Just when I thought she was about to fall asleep, she opened her green eyes and caught me looking at her.

"Ben," she said in the human language. Then, "I love you."

The words had tumbled out dreamily, just when I thought she'd abandoned all her fairy nonsense. I looked at her as if she'd just stolen my mackerel.

"*Love* is one of those strange human concepts," I said. I spoke in the cat language, but I still said 'love' in the human one, because cats didn't even have a word for it.

Ta'ra blinked her eyes as if in disbelief. For a moment, she looked like she wasn't going to argue with me, and would just try to get some more sleep. But then she clearly decided that she had a point to make.

"*Love* is not just known among humans," Ta'ra pointed out. "There's fairies, and pigeons, and dolphins, and many other creatures who experience it."

"How do you know?" I asked.

"Because they stay together for life," Ta'ra said. "And they mourn long after their partner has gone."

"But still," I said. "Cats don't feel it."

Ta'ra turned away from me. She slid a little further towards the edge of the bed giving me room to stretch out a little more.

"What's the matter with you?" I asked.

"I just – I didn't mean to say it. It came out in my sleep."

"Yet still, you said it."

"Well, are you telling me you don't feel it?"

"No," I said.

"Then you must feel something like it. You tell me that you want to live with me forever. You tell me that you can't think of having any other *companion*. You tell me that you think about me a lot, and you always want to spend time with me."

"That's because it's as you said, you're my *companion*. And it's only because you won't let me have any other *companions* that I remain solely by your side."

"Is it really?" Ta'ra asked, raising her voice a little. "If it was really so important to you, then you would have found a *companion* who doesn't mind. Maybe if not Esme, then Geni. Isn't she a fine figure of a Manx, fit for the legendary Dragoncat?"

Seramina whistled aloud in her sleep, then she murmured something. Most of it was incomprehensible, but she mentioned something about *Cana Dei*. Her eyebrows fluttered and for a moment I thought she was going to wake up. Instead, she turned over so that she was facing the wall.

"Look, it's late," I said. "And we really need get some sleep."

Ta'ra yawned. Her teeth looked much sharper than they used to as well. She really was a fine example of a cat. "Look, I don't need you to tell me that you *love* me. It's just a word after all. I just want to know . . ." She trailed off.

"What?"

"I want to know that you really care about me. I want to know that I'll be the last thought on your mind when you die. Because you'll be the last on mine."

"Oh not you as well," I said. "We're going to defeat the warlocks and we're all going to survive this."

"I hope so," Ta'ra said. "But just in case we don't—"

"Then I promise," I interrupted. "That you'll be the last thing I think about."

Ta'ra seemed to like this, and she stalked back over to me and cuddled up next me. We were warm, comfortable, and drowsy, even though we knew the perils that lay ahead of us.

Love. The word came back into my head just before I drifted off to sleep. If this is what it felt like to humans and fairies and all those other creatures Ta'ra had referred to, then perhaps it wasn't such a bad thing after all.

35

BATTLEFIELD

A crash of thunder woke me. I sprang up on Seramina's bed, and my head banged into Ta'ra's. We both yowled at once and then looked at each other, then turned to Seramina who was sitting on the edge of the bed. She wasn't wearing that chiffon dress of hers anymore, but a white robe tied with a rope at the front, just like the white mages wore. She already had her staff strapped to her back.

"It's time," a voice said in my head, with that beautiful Welsh-like lilt to it. *"The battle must commence."*

Seramina nodded to us, then she walked over to her bedroom door and opened it. It was strange; I had expected the room to fill with light. But instead beyond that doorway was the usual darkness of the Fifth Dimension, a pink glow suffusing everything. Except now, streaks of purple also sliced through the darkness. If we didn't move fast enough, the warlocks' magic would tear all this apart.

Seramina strode out, and Ta'ra and I sprinted around her legs and out into Bastet's lair. Already, a portal yawned out of the darkness. Cats, dragons, unicorns, humans, and a dog sat staring out at it. Bastet also watched the portal, keeping quite a distance between herself and it, though she was close enough to not get destroyed by the purple temporal storm.

From it drifted the most disgusting stench of rotten vegetable juice I had ever smelled. It was worse than a midden, and I was surprised nobody had fainted because of it.

Beyond the portal lay the grey barren terrain of the Darklands, with a glowing mist filling the space all around it. The mushroom field was there just as we'd seen in Bastet's simulation of the golems. Above it all, on a steep dark hill, stood the Warlocks' tower, seeming to vanish into to the purple clouds that roiled above it. If I focused hard enough, I could see the outlines of the seven-spoked stone platform within the clouds, rotating slowly. A bright purple light marked the centre of the platform, no doubt coming from the Grand Crystal, which was ready to break the worlds.

The dragons stood on a knoll just to the right of the portal, whilst the unicorns stood on lower ground to the left. The humans and Max were already mounted on their dragons. I noticed that Asinda, atop Shadorow, was wearing a similar robe to Seramina's. Bastet must have handed them out to both of them, and I wondered if Esme and I would have to wear them too.

The cats filled the space between the dragons and the unicorns. I caught sight of Salanraja's ruby scales among the dragons. She turned her head towards me.

"*Our allies' army will be here soon, Bengie,*" she said. "*Then it's time to fly.*"

"*I know,*" I said.

"*So go and join Esme in ordering your cats onto their dragons. You're their commander, remember. They will follow your lead now.*"

I hadn't noticed the pink-nosed alabaster furred Abyssinian standing on a patch of raised earth just in front of the portal. I turned to Ta'ra and brushed my nose against hers.

"Join the others," I said. "We will fly soon."

She sprinted with me over to the clowder. But while she stopped at the rear of them, I carried onwards and jumped onto the ledge next to Esme.

"There you are," Esme said, turning to me. "You took your time, Dragoncat."

"I had some sleeping to do," I said. "And I've not even had time for a good groom."

"You'll have plenty of time for that when we've defeated the warlocks."

"Well, at least one of us believes it."

"Of course I do. We have Seramina, don't we?"

I considered telling her that we might not be able to rely on Seramina as much as we thought we could, but at the end of the day I didn't see a point. We were either going to win or we weren't.

Besides, Esme had already turned her attention towards the unicorns' feline riders, whom she'd trained up beneath her. The street cats of Cimlean City all looked mighty confident. Clearly, Esme had done a good job.

"There's no time for speeches," she said. "But it is exactly as we've discussed. Now mount your unicorns."

As soon as she uttered the last syllable of the final word, the street cats leaped into action. They charged towards their desig-nated unicorns and sprang even higher than they had before onto their mounts. Esme looked so proud.

Exactly as we've discussed, Esme had said. I wondered if there was some kind of speech I should have given to my subordinates to boost their morale. But I guessed Rex had already done all that. Certainly, the cats below me looked ready for battle. A little agitated perhaps, many of them occasionally scratching at their ears with their hind paws. But still they had lowered themselves onto their haunches and were ready to move.

"I'm waiting for your command, Ben," Esme whispered in the human language, to be doubly sure the cats wouldn't hear her.

"Aren't you going to lead the unicorns?" I asked.

"No," she said. "I've given the Persian, Bruno, that job. I'm with the dragon riders. We need to fly up to the stone platform, remember."

I turned to see that Seramina had made it over to her place amongst the dragons. She found her charcoal dragon, Hallinar, and mounted him. Bellari spotted her, and she sidled her citrine dragon, Pinacole, closer to Seramina. She seemed to be assessing her with a watchful eye.

"Okay," I said, and I yowled out at the top of my voice in the cat language: "Dragon riders, mount your dragons. But don't take off until I say the word."

"*More like don't take off before Olan or Corralsa give the word,*" Salanraja said in my mind, and she sounded slightly offended. "*We dragons are in control of our own wings, you know.*"

I ignored her, and instead basked in the elation of the cats replying with yowls of their own. They weren't unfriendly yowls – rather they were feline war cries that we'd developed as a team to spur each other into action.

Esme surged past me, picking up speed as if she saw it as a challenge to reach her dragon first. Before the cats even had a chance to climb the hill where the dragons stood, she was scurrying up Gratis' tail and steadying herself on her dragon's back.

I decided that I should also sprint myself, to show the other cats what a mighty Bengal I was. I had, after all, inherited a powerful set of legs from my great Asian leopard cat ancestors, and I intended to put them to good use.

Though I didn't beat Rex or Geni or Ta'ra or a dozen of the other cats, I still made my way through the clowder and got onto Salanraja's back pretty fast. I was out of breath when I reached her head, but still I felt powerful. If my father, the mighty George, had seen then he would have stirred in his grave.

I peered onwards at the land beyond the portal, still shrouded in purple yuckiness. Apart from the motion of the mist and clouds, and the faint trace of the platform rotating around the tower, there seemed to be little movement. It was as if the land was waiting for us, and we were waiting too.

Suddenly, the first blinks of our allies' forms appeared on the horizon. The White Mages had regrouped and had found ways to summon portals. Several of them yawned open across the land-scape, displaying much more verdant lands on the other side. The purple mist floated towards these, as if it desired to suffocate all life that lived in Illumine Kingdom, where the portals led.

Out of the portals came our allies: dragons soared through the sky, unicorns pounded over the grey earth; regular cavalry on regular horses streamed out from other portals. Then came more foot soldiers, some of them carrying shields, others bows, and others drums that they'd soon be beating to spur us all onwards.

From behind us came a yowl from Bastet louder than any of us mortal cats could yowl. At the front of our formation, Olan and Corralsa let out mighty roars. A couple of the unicorns also responded with loud whinnies.

Then we were flying and charging. Around us, giant white hands appeared in the sky, staff bearers placing our staffs within our mouths. The few humans amongst us also drew their staffs from their backs.

Soon, we and our allies stretched out from expanse to expanse. It was time for the fabled battle that would make history to commence.

36

ARMIES

Our dragons landed together on the ground in front of the portal Bastet had summoned, between the Fifth Dimension and the First, just as it winked shut behind us. The other portals that the White Mages, Dragon Guard, and the king's soldiers had summoned from Illumine Kingdom had also closed. This left our armies facing the Warlocks' Tower with no means of retreat. But that was how it had to be.

This would be the battle that would decide it all. I smelled horses, and dragons, and sweat and fear, and rotten vegetable juice above them all.

A similar storm as that we'd encountered in the Fifth Dimension thundered around us. There was no rain – for I don't think there ever was much water in the Darklands. But still the sky flashed with purple lightning, and my fur stood on end as I imagined the fabric of space-time being wrenched apart.

A bright glow came from the clouds above the tower, and I knew that there was some powerful magic going on up there. If we didn't move soon, the warlocks and *Cana Dei* would end us all.

Regular foot soldiers took the vanguard of our army, holding bossed blue tower shields with silver crosses emblazoned on their fronts. They had these ready to create a protective wall against anything that might try to break through to the army's rear.

Two platoons of cavalry formed either flank of this shield wall. The left was mounted on regular horses, all of them looking strong and ready for war. On the right stood the King's White Guard, and the woman I'd known as Lieutenant Carmista now held the banner that denoted her as captain.

Two lines of archers spanned the width behind the soldiers, and behind them stood the army's drummers, equipped with massive bass drums and smaller snares.

At the back stood the King's Dragon Guard, and amidst these dragons I could also see those I recognised from Dragonsbond Academy. Three large dragons stood out in particular, namely the ruby dragon Flue, the sapphire dragon Farago and the emerald dragon Plishk. These massive dragons belonged to the Council of Three, and the three elders – Yila, Lonamm, and Brigel – sat atop them.

It appeared every single able creature who served the king and could fight had joined our army today. I guessed we needed all the help we could get, because beneath the tower and between the stalks of the mushroom forest, I could faintly make out the warlocks' magical creations waiting for us. Hidden in the mist was the spectral glow of manipulators, and even smaller bright points of the crystals that formed the hearts of golems. Given the warlocks had the upper hand, they didn't need to attack if we didn't. They were simply there to prevent us interrupting the warlocks' spell.

I sat on Salanraja's back facing the dragons. Aleam was on Olan to my left, and Max was on Corralsa to my right. The huge white and black dragons were to command the others, and my job was to orchestrate the movements of the dragon riding cats.

Now the cats sat on the heads of their dwarf dragons, their staffs clasped in their mouths. The land around us was grey and gloomy, which made their eyes seem to shine, every one focused on me.

We stood on a slight hill, looking down into a valley that contained the street cats of Cimlean City, all of them mounted on their unicorns. I don't know how they did it, really. I couldn't stand being anywhere near a horse, even if the beasts were magical. I don't know how the cats managed to sit on top of them, their tails swishing as they whickered away amongst themselves. But then I hadn't grown up with unicorns roaming my neighbouring streets the way Bruno had his comrades had.

"*I'm so proud,*" Salanraja said, examining the dragons in front of us. "*I never thought that I'd stand between the great Olan and the marvellous Corralsa and command a whole platoon of dragons.*"

"Dwarf dragons," I pointed out. "*And it's only because you are bonded to the mighty Dragoncat, descendant of the great Asian leopard cat and the mighty George, eluder of* Cana Dei, *and commander of all cats who ride dragons.*"

"*So your resume lengthens,*" Salanraja said. "*And you always seem to think that you have time to recite it all. Someday something's going to cut you off in mid-sentence, and then you're going to regret it.*"

I growled at her. "*Speaking of which, I never had a chance to use that line to gain the respect of all the Dragoncats before me.*"

"*Oh, please don't,*" Salanraja said, examining one of her foreleg talons.

I didn't have a chance this time either, because from the rearguard of the army that stretched out to our side, the drummers began to beat their drums.

Boom-da-da-da-da. It was the bass drums that said, "boom", and the snare drums that said, "da". Instinctively, every single cat present flattened their ears against their heads. In practice, drumbeats were meant to help everyone keep time. But they just made a racket that we all hated.

I turned to see the massive mushrooms in the fungal forest towering high above us, and the warlocks' tower looming even taller than that. The edges of the floating, rotating stone platform glimmered at the top of it all, reflecting the radiance coming from the purple clouds that enshrouded it.

That was our ultimate target, and our dragons would have to fly through the glowing spores that filled the forest to get there. We would have to cast our magic to stop the dragons from breathing in the noxious fumes that could bring them down out of the sky.

"Archers," called a loud voice from the ranks, clearly augmented by magic. "Loose!"

The fire mages in the dragons' ranks had already stepped forwards. They used their red-crystalled staffs to cast out pillars of flame in front of the archers at the exact time that the archers released the strings of their bows. The burning fire arrows sailed, landing in the mushroom forest, igniting some of the fleshy material and extinguishing spores.

Three more volleys were fired this way, and then there came a succession of booms from the drummers.

There came a scream from the ranks of both cavalry wings: "Charge!"

The horses and unicorns surged forwards. At the same time, fire golems unveiled themselves from within the mushroom forest. They launched themselves as projectiles towards the foot soldiers, covering the sky with flame. The soldiers raised their shields in response.

While all this was happening, five horrific winged figures lifted off from the ground in the distance. They approached us, gaining speed, and it wasn't long before I recognised the craggy forms of demon dragons. They were amongst the most terrifying demons amongst all the creatures in the Seventh Dimension, and they were heading right towards us.

37

BATTLE

The ground beneath our dragons' feet roared with the thunder of both unicorn and regular horse hoofs. In the ranks of the larger cavalry squadron that didn't include cats, the unicorns charged ahead of the regular horses.

Last time I'd seen an army filled with White Mages, they'd had all kinds of magical creatures in it, including chimeras and badger-armadillo-like animals that rolled over the ground attacking their enemies. None of these were present under Carmista's command, and I guess the reason had something to do with Alliander's powerful magic.

Still, her charge performed well. The tails of the riders' white robes streamed behind them as they charged, almost covering the tails of their unicorns. Both horns and staffs glowed brightly, the staffs held high by each of the White Mages' heads. None of them seemed to need to hold onto their mounts for support.

A fountain of pure white magic surrounded the unicorns as they charged, and then the unicorns lowered their horns and rammed them into manipulators who didn't even have time to prepare their magic.

The regular cavalry followed with their swords swinging. Occasionally I saw a horse or unicorn fall, the rider tumbling into the sea of purple mist. Then I heard a cry from the forest, and both lines of cavalry were sweeping out again in two columns.

Meanwhile, we had our own problems on our side of the battlefield. The demon dragons were charging closer, and would be upon us within minutes. At the same time, a line of manipulators had formed out of crystals scattered on the nearby rim of the mushroom forest. The wispy humanoid creations turned their staffs upwards and summoned into the sky a whole host of bone dragons. Shrill shrieks filled the air.

Beneath us, the cats on their unicorns yowled. They scuffed their rear hoofs, then charged forwards. They went straight towards the manipulators, who continued to feed beams of white energy into the bone dragons.

I already had my staff in my mouth, the crystals along it surging with warming energy. The giant magical hand that was my staff bearer hovered above me, awaiting my instructions.

On either side of me, Corralsa and Olan roared out their commands for the dragons to take off. At the same time, I willed my staff bearer to point a finger towards the bone dragons so every single cat on dragonback would understand our target.

This time, we had no need to dismount and attack the manipulators on foot; we had Bruno and his unicorn riding cats to do that for us. Esme had trained them well, and they also had their staffs in their mouths. A flow of White Magic danced between the crystals on them and their unicorns' horns. Streams of energy danced out of the focal point between the two and hit the manipulators in their very hearts.

Just as soon as the cavalry of unicorn riding cats had defeated the manipulators, our dragons reached the bone dragons. They surged forwards as one unit, clouds of green acid spewing out of their mouths to melt dragon and rider whole.

Hitting them back with a wall of dragonfire would do no good. That tactic wouldn't help us avoid their assault.

I kept my focus on my staff bearer above my head. I directed it to point downwards, direct the dragons to go underneath the acid clouds. Salanraja dived. Gravity rushed against me. I turned to see the other dragons doing the same, a flawless execution of my orders.

Then, I willed my staff bearer to click its fingers, and at the same time I channelled magic into my staff. From our staffs we cast every spell we could think of, other than those which involved dark magic. Beams of white, fire, ice, lightning, and leaf magic hit the bone dragons on their heads.

Our aim was true, and our enemies splintered, or fell, or disintegrated, as the feline White Mages beneath us knocked the last crystals out of the manipulator's hearts.

But still there were the demon dragons, and they were seconds away now. The great craggy flying beasts had cracks containing magma that bubbled beneath their hides. Out of their permanently open mouths, powerful vortices sucked anything that crossed their paths into their fiery insides.

Salanraja jerked to a halt, hovering in the air. Corralsa and Olan fanned out to the side a little. On their backs, Max and Aleam already wielded their staffs, energy pulsing in the crystals.

The space that Corralsa and Olan had made allowed Ta'ra's dwarf white dragon Kada and Asinda's charcoal dragon Shadorow to come in on the left. Equally, Esme's dwarf black dragon Gratis and Seramina's charcoal dragon Hallinar entered on the right.

We all waited for the demon dragons, goading them towards

us. Above me, I willed my staff bearer to gesture a wavy line with its palm.

As soon as we felt the first tug, trying to draw us into the great gaping mouths of the demon dragons, our dragons dived down once again. The demon dragons barrelled past us, but the dragons behind us had already fanned out on my staff bearer's command.

I felt my stomach turn as Salanraja twisted in the air to perform a one-eighty. The dragons on either side of us did the same, and we were soon on the demon dragons' tails. For a long time we'd all thought these infernal beasts immortal. But I'd managed to destroy them before, using my own magic. Recently the others had latched onto my methods.

Aleam first unleashed his lightning magic: he summoned up a great storm cloud that slowed the demon dragons and confused their motion somewhat. Once a few bolts had struck their craggy hides, the five of us let out intense beams of White Magic.

It didn't matter if the magic we cast upon them was white or dark; it just mattered that we had power thrumming through us, gifted to us by the crystals. And we had to put all our focus into it, every single morsel of training that we had gathered over the years.

Five beams of intense energy each hit the flanks of a single demon dragon. Welts grew on their sides, like rock melting into a volcano. The demons let out intense roars that threatened to down the dragons that surrounded them. They sounded like boulders crashing against boulders, intended to instil fear into their enemies.

They exploded as one into five massive shards of molten rock. Everywhere, dragons dived out of the way to avoid the flying magma. Then a chorus of feline yowls sang through the air.

We had done it, we had defeated our foes, clearing a path for Seramina, Asinda, Esme, and me – Bastet's loyal Guardians of the White – to approach the stone platform.

38

THROUGH THE CURTAIN

Together, our dragons turned towards the target.

Nobody was to land on the rotating platform except Seramina, Asinda, Esme and me. We were the only ones who knew how to resist *Cana Dei,* should the warlocks try to implant it into our minds. Anyone else could easily and unwittingly become its thrall.

We approached on our dragons, a thick curtain of mist veiling the stone platform so we could only see its edges like blades of a fan slowly cutting through turbid water.

The other dragons kept close enough to us that they could provide support in case the warlocks had posted any more enemies way up high. Anticipation gripped my throat as we approached the edge.

Everything was so thick down there that I couldn't see what lay on the other side of the mist. It also absolutely stank, and part of me thought I was going to throw up. I could taste bile at the back of my throat.

In the centre of it all, like a shining nimbus at the core of a nebula, we could see the Grand Crystal sending out waves of energy.

The storm continued to boil in the sky around us, streaks of purple lightning tearing it apart. Beneath us the battle loomed. I could hear it, but I couldn't tell if we were winning or losing. All I could see were the evil clouds drifting below. Beneath that, tendrils of *Cana Dei* were spreading out, as if probing their way into new life.

We were almost at the edge, and our dragons lifted their claws, ready to land. Some dragons approached closer than the others. They belonged to Bellari, Ange, and Rine.

Bellari had Pinacole positioned slightly ahead of the other two, who were looking at her as if wondering what in the Seventh Dimension she was up to. But the dragons seemed to know – clearly they had communicated plans of their own amongst themselves.

"It's time, Bengie," Salanraja said as she slowed her wings.

"For once, please, can you call me Ben? This could be the last time you speak to me."

"Then make sure you come back, and I'll grant your request."

"Oh you are so . . ."

"What?"

"Just shut up, will you?"

"Now that's a wish I can grant right now." And she did, much to my relief.

Together the dragons turned in a motion we'd rehearsed long before. Their tails swished, then curled down towards the rim of the platform as it turned to meet them.

We were ready; Seramina was the only one likely to stumble, as Esme and I were cats and Asinda was built like a monkey.

I timed it perfectly, charging down Salanraja's tail. She stiffened it at the last moment, then gave it a flick to propel me forwards. I dived through the clouds, sensing the other three falling besides me. I hit cold stone and I rolled.

I passed through a freezing wall of gaseous rotten vegetables. It was noxious, and I thought it would burn my lungs from the inside. But I got to the other side, and when I did, everything seemed clear.

I lifted myself to see the immensity of the stone platform. It seemed much larger inside the purple cloud-dome of dark magic that surrounded it.

But I didn't have much of a chance to look around, because we had inadvertently stumbled upon the spoke that hosted Alliander in her human form. She wasn't feeding dark magic into the crystal the way the other warlocks and the crocodile-hippopotamus-lion demon goddess Ammit were.

Instead she had clearly been expecting us, her staff clenched tight in both hands and the fires of *Cana Dei* burning at the back of her eyes.

39

THE STONE PLATFORM

"You have thirty seconds to admire our work," Alliander said. "Then, traitors, you shall die."

She hadn't spoken in the voice of the Captain of the White Guards that I'd come to know so well. Instead, she spoke in the deep, sonorous, rumbling voice of *Cana Dei*, with a sharpness to it that grated against the walls of my ear canals like chalk against a board.

Thirty seconds wasn't much, but I needed at least a little time to understand the environment in which we were to fight this battle.

Behind Alliander, the Grand Crystal floated in the air – except it no longer resembled the Grand Crystal that I'd known before. Instead, it was surrounded by purple mist, and had so many cracks in its surface that it looked like it might split apart should the magic fail to hold it together. The crystal glowed bright purple, as the warlocks continued to feed energy into it.

I could see how each of the warlocks stood on a rune at the end of their designated platforms, the etched sigils glowing beneath their feet. The crystal blocked our view of Ammit, who was standing on the lonely spoke opposite Alliander's. The Grand Crystal had a white halo behind it, with red light filling the space between that and the crystal. It didn't take me long to realise that a portal to the Seventh Dimension must have been opened somewhere on Ammit's spoke.

Alongside the rotten stench of dark magic I could also smell brimstone. The fact that the portal was open meant any demons could flood out of it, at Ammit's beck and call. I had little doubt that this had been the source of the five demon dragons whom we had battled before.

Beneath the Grand Crystal, in the hole that should have looked down into the turret of the warlocks' tower, lay an inky pool of darkness, and from it emanated another smell of yeast extract. It took me only a moment to realise that I was looking through a portal into the Ghost Realm, the Third Dimension. Except there were no blue outlines, only the dark shadowy form of *Cana Dei,* streaks of it seeping towards the corners between the crystal's facets.

Whiskers. They were summoning *Cana Dei* directly into the Grand Crystal, just as Bastet had said they would. But that wasn't what had alarmed me. It was the sudden realisation that the Grand Crystal had a connection to the other crystals – from here, *Cana Dei* could find its way into every single source of magic that we had.

Our staffs. The unicorns' horns. Each dragon's breath. It would all come under the command of *Cana Dei.* The warlocks and Ammit wouldn't break the world alone; instead, it was the crystals that would do so, destroyed from the inside out.

"Time's up," Alliander said, and a quick pulse of light in the crystal at the end of her staff followed her words.

A beam of energy shot out so fast that I almost missed it. But my instinct had been trained through so many months of using magic – without even having to think about it, a beam came from my staff to meet hers. Purple and white energy clashed, a globe of magic swelling at the contact point. Then she cut it out.

All of a sudden, I felt a twisting in the gut, just as the fires in Alliander's eyes flared for a moment.

I tried to continue the spell, but I found myself unable. Alliander had cut off my magic.

"Very good," she said, continuing in the voice of *Cana Dei*. "What about the—" a bolt of energy shot out of her staff heading straight for Asinda "—daughter of the Warlock Prince."

Asinda also had lightning reflexes, her magical energy matching Alliander's. But the spell went out just as it had with me, and so did Asinda's ability to cast it.

"Let's try Magecat," Alliander said.

Her purple magical beam shot straight towards Esme this time. The Abyssinian met it with a greater flourish than Asinda or I had mustered. But this time I heard a loud pop, and again her magic went out.

"What is happening?" Esme said. "This is impossible."

Alliander ignored her. Instead she turned her fiery gaze on Seramina. "All this time, you've had the opportunity to strike me down. I expected you to lash out first and try to end it. I anticipated you'd challenge the force that almost consumed you."

As Alliander spoke, I was trying my hardest to will energy into my staff. But some strange and unexpected twist in *Cana Dei's* magic had sapped my abilities. I considered turning into a chimera to charge at her, but I found even my muscles unable to move. I realised then that I was rooted to the spot, almost paralysed.

"Alliander," Seramina said. "I know that you're trapped in there somewhere. I know how it feels to be taken by the darkness – to become lost in there – but you can fight it."

Alliander cackled with laughter. Except the voice didn't belong to the version of her that Seramina was trying to reach. Every part of Alliander that we saw before us was all the work of *Cana Dei*.

The fires continued to burn brightly in the former White Mage Captain's eyes. The rotten vegetables now smelled like scorched rotten vegetables. Esme, Asinda, and I still found ourselves unable to move.

"If you really want to try to save me, then you will have to do so metal to metal," Alliander said.

Her crystal flared bright lilac, and a powerful and searing beam came out of it. It was targeted straight at Seramina's heart, as if *Cana Dei* wanted to find a route straight into her soul.

Seramina swung her staff around and met the beam with a hot white one of her own. The bulb of energy flared like a miniature sun at the centre of their beams, hanging there for a moment.

"Listen to me," Seramina said. I could see the muscles in her hands straining. "That voice you hear in your head, Alliander, it isn't you. If you just learn to shut off your mind, then it will harm you no longer."

"Is that right?" *Cana Dei* said through Alliander's mouth. "Are you telling me that you're too scared to destroy her?"

Seramina, what are you doing? I asked in my head. But I couldn't find a way to open my mouth and voice the question. I tried to reach out to Salanraja, to at least get her to try and communicate through Hallinar. But even that channel seemed to be blocked.

"I'm not scared," Seramina replied. "I feel only compassion. And I know that you can be saved."

For a moment, the blossoming bulb of energy at the centre of the beams travelled closer to Alliander. For an instant, it looked as if Seramina might win.

"So do it," Alliander said, a wicked grin upon her face. "Kill me. End it all . . ."

"No," Seramina said. "I can save you. Just close your mind to your thoughts and open yourself to peace. That's how I learned to do it in the end. That's what I did to keep it out."

A grimace appeared on Alliander's face and for a moment I wondered if the teenager was getting through to her. The bulb of energy hovered right in front of her, and I realised that Seramina was holding it there. For a very brief moment, the fires faded from Alliander's eyes.

"There you are," Seramina said, her eyes studying Alliander carefully. "Now let us save the others."

I saw Seramina's magic dwindle, and the confluence of pure energy fell back towards the centre between them. She had reduced the power from her staff, giving Alliander room to also ease off.

At that moment, the fire returned to Alliander's eyes. She clenched her fists around her staff, and the beam coming out of her staff swelled with even more energy. It was so powerful that it pushed back the bulb along the two beams like a spark travelling down a wire.

It hit Seramina hard on the chest, and she dropped her staff.

"No," she uttered, ever so faintly. Then she stumbled and fell to the floor. The life went out of her eyes.

"Seramina," I said.

Somehow, I managed to find the energy to call her name, but the word came out weakly.

Alliander glanced at me, then turned her attention back to the girl and sighed.

"Such a coward," she said. "Now the rest of you must receive the mark of death."

She turned her attention towards Asinda first, but a flash of motion caught her eye above her, approaching from behind. It took all my strength to do so, but I managed to look over my shoulder to see a citrine dragon diving through the curtain of mist.

Bellari was astride him, her legs crouched on her dragon's head ready to jump off. She held her staff in her hands, and the crystal at its head blazed with virgin fire.

40

THE ULTIMATE FIRE MAGIC

Fires raged at the back of Alliander's eyes, and the eyebrows above them had furrowed into a curious frown. She watched the dragon approach, her head cocked. Standing on the citrine dragon Pinacole's head, Bellari had her staff clutched tightly in her hands.

Weakened by Alliander's – or should I say *Cana Dei's* – magic, I was still unable to move, as were Asinda and Esme. Seramina lay in front of us, lifeless on the floor.

Bellari swiftly jumped off her mount as the dragon circled around. Just before he turned away from us, I saw sadness in his eyes. But still I hadn't worked out what he and Bellari were up to.

"Bellari, come back!" Rine shouted from his mount, the emerald Ishtkar. "You can't fight *Cana Dei*."

The golden-blonde teenager turned back to her fiancé. "I love you, Rine," she shouted back. "My heart is yours!"

Rine crawled up to Ishtkar's head as if he were ready to jump onto the platform himself. But his dragon wouldn't let him anywhere near it. On the sapphire dragon Quarl's back, Ange watched him cautiously, Palimali sitting behind her thrashing her tail. Though the desert cheetah seemed oblivious, it was clear Ange was in on this too.

A memory flashed back into my mind of stepping in front of Asinda, of stopping her from saving Lars. Now Ange and Ishtkar had needed to make that same decision with Rine. Because I'd realised his fiancée was about to sacrifice herself, though I still didn't quite know what she planned to achieve.

Alliander cast no magic against Bellari; instead her mouth twisted into a sideways grin.

"What are you up to, foolish girl?" she asked.

"Do you know of the ultimate fire magic?"

"The what?" Alliander's eyes registered surprise, then recognition dawned in her eyes. Purple mist started to rise around her, and tiny feathers grew out of her hands and shoulders.

"The ultimate fire magic," Bellari said again.

The crystal at the top of her staff was glowing like the brightest possible magma. But she wasn't casting any magic at Alliander. Instead she channelled the fire into herself.

"Sacrifice," Bellari said. "An act your kind has never known."

"Such a fool," Alliander said. "There's no way you can defeat us."

A sudden explosion of purple smoke billowed out around the former White Mage Captain, concealing her from view. This quickly expanded, the clouds forming into massive feathers, which again transformed into horrific looking snakes.

The mighty griffin stood before us with a lion's face and two powerfully clawed talons, and it launched into the air.

"You're perfectly right," Bellari said. "I can't defeat you all . . . but Seramina can."

Her skin had gone bright crimson, like the worst allergy she'd ever had. Fire now surrounded her, jumping out of her skin and clothes and back into them again like solar flares. These flames then took on a shape of their own, like feathers of fire. Heat surged out of her, letting out a smell akin to woodsmoke.

"Behold the power of the phoenix!" she screamed.

And those were the last words she uttered, because the firebird separated from her body, launching up into the air to meet the griffin head on. Meanwhile, the girl Bellari's eyes had gone white, and she collapsed onto the floor.

"Bellari, no!" Rine called from beyond the platform. "Let me down there!" He had his staff drawn and was brandishing it. Quarl had moved into Rine's path, and Ange also had her staff drawn, as if ready to block off any of his magic.

From the massive lion's mouth above us, the griffin that was Alliander let out a roar. It shook the stone platform under our feet, making it feel as if it might topple.

At the same time, the phoenix which had grown to the same massive size as the griffin, gave out its own cry. Its voice sounded like a raging inferno, and the firebird extended two mighty talons of fire.

The birds met in a flurry of feathers and claws. Screeches and cries and roars filled the sky. Purple lightning raged in the distance, accompanied by crashes of thunder. Above, the purple clouds surrounding the griffin and the red flames surrounding the phoenix seemed to lash out against each other, as if they had lives of their own.

Suddenly, the griffin turned upwards, and then it spun around as if ready to drive its beak into the firebird's flank. At the same time the phoenix charged forward, its flaming beak closing over the griffin's neck.

There came the loudest crash of thunder from the storm of them all, and an intense flash of lightning. Then the griffin was falling, spearing down back towards the platform. Just before it hit the stone, it halted as if repelled by some kind of magic.

Another ball of purple mist gathered around Alliander's body. Then it faded quickly, revealing the White Mage captain lying lifeless on the stone, dressed in her white robe. Her staff lay next to her, discarded on the ground.

"Bellari!" Rine screamed again, his gaze now focused on the phoenix. "Return her life to her."

But the phoenix wasn't focused on Bellari now. Rather, it dived straight down towards Seramina, shrinking as it gathered speed. Flames wrapped around its slender body, and it plunged straight into Seramina's chest, where her heart was.

Seramina's eyes shot open, just as Bellari's body gave one last shudder and fell limp.

The silver-haired teenager stood up, and at the same time the weakness faded from my muscles. Asinda and Esme also seemed to have recovered, and we moved to stand near Seramina.

Together we looked back at Bellari, lying there helpless, her face now pale white. She had sacrificed herself to save us all, and in doing so she'd given us exactly what we needed to win.

41

EXUDING CONFIDENCE

N ow that the threat had passed, Ange's dragon Quarl moved aside to let Ishtkar and Rine land on the stone platform. He dismounted, and rushed forward, sobbing. He checked for a pulse on Bellari's neck, and then he collapsed over her body, waves of grief wracking through his body.

Esme, Asinda and I had moved closer to Seramina, who watched Rine with tears on her lower eyelids. "Did she?"

"The ultimate fire magic," Asinda said. "She summoned the power of the phoenix."

Seramina lowered her head, and then looked back towards the Grand Crystal. It still hovered above the central axis of the stone platform. The warlocks and their demon were still channelling magic into it, the cracks on its surface growing ever deeper. It seemed that they no longer needed Alliander and her connection to White Magic to break the worlds.

Seramina's eyes became narrow slits. She clenched her fists by her sides and exhaled a heavy breath, then she quickly swooped her staff back up off the ground and turned back to face the glowing purple crystal.

"Let's end this," she said, and I could already see the change in her.

All of a sudden, she seemed less the teenager who didn't know her place in the world, and more the vision of her future I'd seen in the Ghost Realm. She was no longer the girl that *Cana Dei* could use to break the worlds and then discard like a used toy. Instead she exuded confidence, and she exuded hope – a leader to us all.

She clutched her hands around her staff. There came a flash of light, and then there were five of her. Not glamours, but something else. I could smell the snowdrop perfume on each and every version of her. She had summoned some powerful magic from within to do this, magic that I hadn't even known existed.

But then it didn't seem strange to any of us. We'd all known for a long time that she had more innate power within her than any magician we'd ever encountered.

"I will deal with the warlocks," she said. "You three must face Ammit."

All five Seraminas sprinted in separate directions. She moved as fast as my ancestors had, the great Asian leopard cats whom I'd met in the Third Dimension. I don't know what she did, but after a few moments, the beams feeding the crystal from the five adjacent spokes went out.

Esme, Asinda and I looked at each other. We exchanged nods and just before we were about to run to the other side of the platform, a voice came from behind us.

"Oh no, Ben. You're not battling any more demons without me."

I turned to first see the white dwarf dragon Kada hovering above the edge of the stone platform. Below him, I caught a glint in Ta'ra's green eyes. She licked her lips, displaying her splendid pair of teeth.

"Ta'ra," I said. "It's—"

"Don't try to tell me that it's too dangerous for me, because I can fight just as well as you can. You've defeated Alliander, I see. Now you can do with an extra ally."

I wanted to object, but she looked as if she'd kill me if I said anything more.

"Come on," Esme said. "We haven't got much time."

We sprinted around the Grand Crystal, Ta'ra summoning her staff bearer as we went. Then we three cats had our staffs in our mouths, energy surging within them. Asinda held hers in her left hand.

Ammit awaited us on the other side, a demon staff bearer hovering above her. As soon as she saw us approach, Ammit studied us intently, then she clacked her crocodile jaws.

Behind her, from the great gaping portal that opened into the Seventh Dimension, demons of every kind were falling from the sky.

42

THE BELLY OF A
HIPPOPOTAMUS

I'd only met a demon who could rival Ammit's size once before, namely the Overlord of Overlords, the demon snake Apopis. He'd been scary, but Ammit was perhaps the scariest creature I'd ever seen, and it wasn't just because of her craggy skin and the glowing magma that shone out from beneath it.

She had the head of a crocodile and the forepaws of a lion, both of which looking like sharp instruments of death by themselves. She also had a lion's mane that extended from behind her eyes. But what scared me more was her powerful rear body.

Back home in the Fourth Dimension, my two neighbourhood Savannah Cats had always said that the worst death, the one to fear amongst all others, happens beneath the belly of the hippopotamus. Since they both had the mighty serval as their ancestor that would have had to face hippopotamuses every day, they had an authority on this matter.

Thus, despite Ammit's clacking jaws and powerful forelegs, it was the sight of the rest of its body that sent a shudder through me.

It made me wonder if the Savannah Cats' stories had been portents of my own demise, for that's what I was staring at: the hindquarters of a hippopotamus. She was so large that she could leap upon us and suffocate us all.

Ammit didn't seem to sense my fear, or at least she didn't bother to comment upon it. Rather, her reptilian eyes looked left and right. She must have realised that the other warlocks had stopped *Cana Dei's* spell, because she turned off the beam summoning energy into the Grand Crystal.

Then, it was as if the narrow slits in her green eyes focused on all of us at once.

When she spoke, I had expected to hear the clacking and booming voice of a demon, but instead came that same rumbling and sonorous voice of *Cana Dei*.

"You may have stopped me from breaking the worlds, but I still have my demons and they are quite capable of destroying everything."

"Not if we can help it," Ta'ra said, albeit in a mumbling voice because of the staff in her mouth.

"Oh yeah, and what are you going to do?"

Ta'ra didn't waste a moment. "Butterflies!" she said.

A thick golden spark of lightning came from her staff. It hit Ammit on her crocodilian snout, then it sizzled and evaporated like a splash of water hitting hot rock.

"What, why didn't that work?" Ta'ra asked. "Butterflies!"

She tried again, this time directing the beam at the craggy demon staff-bearer that loomed above us. Again the spell fizzled out, and in the same way.

"You cannot turn a demon into butterflies," *Cana Dei* said.

"Why not?"

"Because demons are immortal and butterflies aren't."

"Whiskers," Ta'ra said, twitching hers.

Asinda took the opportunity to summon some powerful white magic from her staff. A purple beam came out of the staff hovering above Ammit's head to match it.

"You know they called this minion, the bringer of death, the devourer of souls," *Cana Dei* said. "She would have eaten you for breakfast had you met her a thousand years ago when she roamed these lands."

Asinda's muscles in her jaw tensed as she struggled with her staff against Ammit's powerful beam. I could see that she would be overwhelmed within seconds, so I directed a beam of energy at Ammit with my own staff.

I didn't aim to kill. I would need some extremely powerful magic to destroy her like we had the demon dragons. No, it only needed to be strong enough to knock the demon goddess back through the portal. Then we could work out what to do next.

A second beam split off from the beam aiming for Asinda. It hit me like a wrecking ball, and I had to use all the strength in my muscles and mind to push back against it.

Esme shot a third beam at Ammit, and as before the beam coming out of the staff split to meet it.

This took the strain off me a little, but still it was too much. I could feel the sweat pouring out of the glands in my feet. My muscles were failing, and I could taste acid at the back of my throat.

Ammit was just too powerful, and we didn't have Seramina here to help fight her. We could only sustain this for a few seconds, before her magic would scorch us to ash.

Ta'ra growled. "Let me try this one final time," she said. "*Butterflies*." This time she directed her beam of energy at the staff in the demon staff-bearer's hand. She didn't aim for the crystal; she instead went straight for the wood at the centre.

There was a fizzle, a pop, and then a rustle that sounded like wind sighing through a forest. The staff steamed, and then a thousand butterflies of every different colour floated out of it.

"No!" Ammit screamed as our joint magic hit her right within her gaping mouth.

We had put so much effort into it that it sent her tumbling backwards, right through the portal from whence she'd come.

"Does anyone know how to close a portal to the Seventh Dimension?" Esme asked.

"Not me," I said. "Seramina does," I pointed out.

"I have an idea," Ta'ra said. "Portals aren't immortal, so . . . Butterflies, butterflies, butterflies."

The beam that came out of her staff was stronger than the last three had been. Behind the portal, I could already see Ammit readying herself for a charge.

The demon goddess kicked back shards of obsidian from the earth beneath her hindquarters as she quickly accelerated, gathering speed back towards the portal.

But before she could charge back through, the portal shone a bright golden colour, its surface opaque enough to seal Ammit inside. For a moment, it looked like a gilded mirror reflecting the purple mist and the darkness back upon itself.

The portal turned to smoke, and then to thousands upon thousands of golden coloured butterflies. They spiralled around each other and then took off into the sky.

I had no idea where they decided to fly to. I didn't care.

All that mattered was that we had won. We had beaten the warlocks, and we had beaten the great demon crocodile-lion-hippopotamus goddess Ammit.

But still the matter of *Cana Dei* remained.

43

REBIRTH

Wе met the warlocks on the stone platform where we had parted from Seramina, and to the surprise of all of us, they were still alive. They had huddled together right beneath the great crystal, hunched over the fallen body of Alliander. The first thought that came to mind was that they were trying to revive her so they could finish the ritual without Ammit.

Asinda, Esme and I readied ourselves for battle, despite how exhausted we were. But the warlocks had no staffs to defend themselves with, and I caught a glimpse of Seramina crouched down behind them, next to where their staffs lay criss-crossed on the ground.

"Wait," I said in the human language, so Asinda would also understand. "They're not our enemies. Not anymore."

The warlocks turned their heads towards us. Fire no longer burned in their eyes, which expressed nothing but confusion. Each of them looked as if they had just awoken from a thousand-year dream. There were red scars all over their faces where those eggshell-like cracks had been.

"They killed Lars," Asinda said, bitterness in her voice.

"Not them," Esme said. "*Cana Dei.*"

Asinda took a deep breath, her teeth clenched. Then she relaxed and lowered her staff. "You're right," she replied.

I stalked over to Seramina, who had her hand cupped around Alliander's head. The teenager had also lowered her staff on the ground. She turned to me.

"I did it," she said. "I managed to help the warlocks banish *Cana Dei* from their minds. They have agreed to cooperate. They don't remember any of it. It turns out they were possessed by it before they even touched dark magic."

I examined them, the old man Moonz, the red-haired Cala, the thin and wiry Pladana, the bald muscular giant Ritrad, and the lanky Junas. I wondered if they could still transform into their carrion eater forms. But something about the way they gazed distantly told me that they'd lost all their magic. They were now just regular men and women.

I heard Alliander gasping for air from beneath me, and I looked down startled to see her open her eyes. She blinked a few times, taking in her surroundings. Then her eyes fell on Seramina.

"It's you," she said in a weak voice. "You didn't kill me."

Seramina's eyebrows furrowed. "You were the enemy. But now . . . I don't see a trace of *Cana Dei* in you anymore."

Alliander grimaced. "So it did take me."

Seramina nodded. "What do you remember?" she asked.

Alliander propped herself up on her elbows. Then she sat up and shook her head. "When I dropped you off at your residence, I still worried about the warlocks. So I read threads of destiny, and I saw the Grand Crystal, and I saw it explode. I saw exactly what has to happen right now. But I peered in too far, and that's when *Cana Dei* reached in and took control of my mind."

She looked at the ground, running her hand over the rough

stone. Then she seemed to recognise where she was and turned back to look at the crystal. It was pulsing with energy, letting out waves of purple light, heat and smelly gas. I could sense something stirring underneath it's facets. *Cana Dei* was still in there.

"It's too late," Alliander said. "If we don't stop it, it will break the world."

Seramina bowed her head. "I can destroy it," she said. "That's what I must do, right?"

"Do you realise what this means?" Alliander said, and she stood up.

"I do," Seramina said.

"Then it's just as I saw before *Cana Dei* took over my mind. It's necessary, I think."

"I know . . ." Seramina said, and she lifted her staff and strode forwards.

"Wait a minute," I said. "Can someone please explain to me what's going on?"

Alliander looked down at me as she bent down to pick up her staff. "There's no time to explain. Seramina, before you do what you must, where is the girl?"

"Who?" Seramina asked.

"The fire mage?"

Seramina pointed with her staff to where Rine was crouched still slumped over her body. He held her hand in his, and though he didn't show his face, it was clear he was weeping.

Alliander strode over to him, and he looked up as he heard her footsteps.

"I thought you died," Rine said, his eyes red rimmed. He drew the staff from his back. "Bellari sacrificed herself to end you."

"She did," Alliander said. "And her magic purged the *Cana Dei* from me. Now, as long as her blood hasn't yet run cold, I can save her."

"Did you not hear me?" Rine shouted. "She's dead!"

The crystal on his staff started to glow bright blue, tiny shards of ice forming on the surface of it.

Someone put her hand on his shoulder. I looked up to see Quarl hovering above the stone platform behind Rine, with Palimali at her side growling at Rine. Ange wasn't on her dragon's back because she had already dismounted and stepped up to Rine, there to lend a helping hand.

"Trust her, Rine," she said. "I saw what happened from the air. This isn't the enemy we faced."

Rine turned to Ange, and his gaze turned as cold as the crystal on his staff. "You," Rine said, his lips trembling. "If you hadn't blocked my path, I could have stopped her."

I moved over to Rine in hope that I could comfort him in some way. I looked back at Alliander, and I saw nothing but kindness in her eyes.

"Please," Alliander said. "This is how I can put things right again. I know a lot about magic, and so I know how to do this."

Rine looked at Asinda, and she nodded at him and wiped a tear from her cheek with the back of her hand. Rine puffed the air out of his lips, then he stood up and stepped back. Bellari's golden hair framed her pale face.

Alliander looked back at Seramina. "Start the spell," she said. "I have time now."

Seramina nodded, and a sudden beam of light shot out of her staff. It hit the Grand Crystal right on its closest face.

"Wait," Asinda said looked at her then examining her staff. "Does that mean—?"

"Every single crystal will dissolve," Esme said as if reading her thoughts. "We will be able to use magic no more."

Whiskers, I'd hadn't even thought about that. But then it made sense. The warlocks had gathered *Cana Dei* into the heart of the crystals, and now it had no way out. It would also shatter. But it was the only way we could win.

I recalled something I'd learned during my only visit to the Fourth Dimension since I'd moved there.

As Seramina continued to feed energy into the Grand Crystal, Alliander raised her staff above her head, and her staff transformed into one of a fire mage, with a red crystal at its head.

"The ultimate fire magic," she said.

I felt heat burning from her skin, flares dancing out and around her. Her russet hair whipped out, also seeming to be on fire, and then those blazing feathers grew out of her shoulders. Alliander let out a loud scream and the phoenix bloomed out of her, as her body collapsed to the platform.

At the same time there came a sound like a million panes of glass splintering from behind. I spun around to see the crystal shatter, first only into several pieces, then into shards, then into smaller shards, then into particles too small for my eyes to see.

My staff bearer held my staff above my head. My heart lurched as I saw the crystals along the length of it shatter in much the same way. It happened not only to my staff, but to every single staff on the platform save Ta'ra's, which was powered by fairy dust.

I remembered back in the Sahara on that night I'd met Pali-mali, I'd also learned about the demise of the crystals in the Fourth Dimension – my original home. The crystals there had disintegrated into sand because humans had misused them for their power. If they hadn't made that choice, the original Pharoah Warlocks would have destroyed that dimension. Now, it seemed that the crystals had made the same choice in this one.

Thus the realm lost its magic, and we were all transformed from being magicians into regular cats and humans.

At that very same moment, Alliander's phoenix dived down from the sky. It shrank as it gathered speed, accelerating towards

Bellari's chest. It plunged into the point where her heart had once beat, vanishing inside her.

All went silent. The purple clouds around us seemed to drift away. In the distance, there was no sign of lightning flashing in the sky. No thunder boomed, and I couldn't hear the incessant humming of the crystals powering up with magic. The air even took on a slight freshness. It felt normal to breathe again.

Bellari opened her eyes, and her gaze immediately fell on Rine who was looking down upon her lovingly. She smiled, and opened her mouth as if to utter his name. It was at that moment that the stone platform lurched to one side and began to fall.

44

WARGS UNITED

Fortunately, our dragons were ready to catch us from off the stone platform just before it toppled and finally tumbled from off the Warlocks' Tower. Our dragons didn't just carry us away, but took the warlocks too.

Because of Salanraja's corridor of spikes, she couldn't hold any human rider. Ta'ra's and Esme's dwarf dragons weren't strong enough to carry them.

So the five warlocks were distributed amongst Ishtkar, Plishk, Pinacole, Shadorow, and Olan. They sat behind each human dragon rider, scanning the ground beneath them, their faces looking long and tired. Seramina had insisted on carrying Alliander's body on Hallinar. She felt that the former White Mage Captain deserved a proper burial. None of us had argued with that, not even Asinda.

I sat on Salanraja's back and watched as the stone platform fell, creaking as it plummeted through the air. It hit the ground with a loud crash, sending up plumes of dust and pushing out a shockwave that cleared the field of any remaining purple mist.

Even up here, the air seemed to be getting fresher. The sky was clearing; the purple colour had almost left it now, and the layer of grey that had constantly covered the land seemed to be fading to white.

Then, all I could see was the glint of light off the crystals that had once been the hearts of the warlocks' magical creations. There was an army down there too, and I squinted as I recognised the lumbering forms.

The field was full of hunchbacked canine creatures, their backs looking like shifting grey mounds as they scoured the battle-field. I noticed the street cats on their unicorns, sitting not far from the army of wargs. Then my heart lurched as I realised they could no longer use their magic to defend themselves. If those wargs decided to charge them, they were doomed.

"*Salanraja, we need to bring our dragons down and do some-thing about those wargs,*" I said in my mind.

"*Relax, Bengie,*" she said. "*It's already handled. They're on our side.*"

"*I thought you said you'd call me Ben once this was all over. And how can they be on our side?*"

"*I will in due time. Meanwhile, the wargs – can you not see how Max is talking to them.*"

She turned her head towards a black form streaking through the sky on our left. It was Corralsa, and Max was sitting on her back howling. I focused my ears so I could listen to what he was saying in the dog language.

"Follow me my *wargs,*" he howled. "You are my brothers and sisters. You no longer need to serve the evil *Cana Dei.* Now I will lead you to a new home."

The way he pronounced the word 'warg' sounded slightly different to the way he'd been previously using it. After all, he'd always barked it before, and now he voiced the word in a howl.

Salanraja caught me noticing, and she decided to offer an explanation.

"*Corralsa explained it all to me,*" she said. "*Because I have to say I was curious.*"

"*Explained what?*" I asked.

Salanraja chuckled. "*While it appears that your crystal gave you the gift of understanding all languages, it's clear they didn't give you the ability to understand all dialects.*"

"*But he was saying warg all along, how couldn't I understand this?*"

"*No,*" Salanraja said. "*I think you'll find he was in fact saying* 'wark'."

She barked out the final word in her mouth like a dog would bark. Of course, it didn't sound like 'wark' sounds in the human language. I'm just providing the best possible translation.

"*What?*" I asked.

"*Wark,*" Salanraja said. "*It means—*"

"*I know what it means,*" I snapped.

It was a word that neither humans, nor dragons, nor cats have in their languages. I guess it literally translates to something like 'enemy of an infernal nature who poses a threat to myself or my current or future master'. Although even its broad meaning is difficult to express in a language other than dog.

"*You mean all this time, I've been chiding him for mistakenly labelling enemies wargs, and he has been right all along.*"

"*Exactly,*" Salanraja said. "*You've been very cruel to the poor Sussex spaniel.*"

I growled. "*I'm not apologising to him,*" I said.

"*Of course you're not. Cats never apologise to dogs.*"

I had absolutely nothing to say to that. After all, I didn't like to be proven wrong.

Instead, I watched from Salanraja's head as Max rounded up

the wargs on the battlefield and then led them South, away from the Darklands and from Illumine Kingdom, towards their new home. As if to greet him, the clouds parted to display the first sight of blue sky that the Darklands had seen for centuries. Then they parted further, to greet the warm rays of a fresh sun.

45

THE FUNERAL

The early spring sun was shining on the hill south of Cimlean City, sending down a soft and comfortable warmth. It was late morning, and drops of dew hung off the stalks of grass that tickled my paws. The scent of pollen was fresh in the air, and the wind sighed gently overhead, rustling my fur. I hadn't eaten, but I still had the taste in my mouth of the mutton sausages we'd eaten at a campfire last night. This morning, though, it had seemed more appropriate to fast.

Lilacs had started to bloom in the valley below, and bluebells and poppies swayed in the meadows beneath the trees. Swallows occasionally dived down to pluck up insects from the meadow, and the air swirling out of the vale tasted fresh and pure.

I stood next to Ta'ra and in front of two headstones sticking out of the earth. Beneath them, two ebony coffins lay deep within twin holes in the ground. One headstone was made of granite and emblazoned with a border of gold set in floral patterns. Within the border were carved the words, "Driar Lars, commander of the King's Dragon Guard, a hero and friend dear to us all."

The other headstone was made of obsidian with a simple marble border. Carved in the centre and set with silver were the words, "Captain Alliander, hero, leader, beloved protector of the realm."

A path led between the two graves, straight and made of bricks of an intensely red sandstone. Some minerals added to the bricks made them sparkle in the sunlight.

The dragon riders – including the King's Dragon Guard and the Driars and Initiates of Dragonsbond Academy – stood close to Lars' grave.

Asinda was at the front, holding a bunch of red and white roses in one hand that contrasted with her red hair. She held a handkerchief in her other hand close to her face. She wore a black robe tied by a white cord, as did all the human dragon riders.

Between Asinda and a pile of dirt stood Driar Calin, Lars' life-long friend who was bonded to the crippled dragon Galludo. He had a shovel in his hand, ready to lower the dirt on Lars' grave. Our dragons stood looking out from a hill rising behind us. Every single dragon known to the realm was present, including those dwarf dragons who were bonded to the cats, the dragons of Dragonsbond Academy, and the King's Dragon Guard, and at the back of them all the mighty bronze Matharon and his guardians, seeming to tower over the rest of the dragons save perhaps Olan and Corralsa.

I scanned the human crowd to see Seramina standing between Ange and Aleam, a distant gaze in her eyes. Max sat at Seramina's feet, Palimali at Ange's. Next to them, Rine and Bellari had their hands interlaced, their backs ramrod straight. Warm gazes and smiles passed between them, but still I could see the sadness in their eyes.

All of the dragon riding cats were here too, and I'd instructed them not to chase any butterflies or other spring insects that might fly their way. I had worried that some of them might not listen, but apparently Rex and Esme had also given them stern warnings. They were thus still and silent, though I did see many cats doze off during the ceremony multiple times.

The White Mages stood near Alliander's grave, wearing their standard white robes, except this time tied with a black cord. The newly appointed Captain Carmista of the White Guard held the flowers, for Alliander a bunch of white lilies and pink orchids. The bald-headed and youthful looking Lieutenant Larmend stood by the patch of dirt above Alliander's grave, a shovel in his hands.

At the back of the crowd, the five former warlocks also watched the funeral. Each of them had been interrogated many times by multiple members of the White Guard, and the results had been communicated to everyone who served under the king, including those of us still in training at the academies.

There came a murmur from the procession, then King Garmin emerged at the foot of the sandstone path. He wore a black doublet, breeches of the same colour, and a red robe that trailed behind him as he walked the space between the two graves.

He stopped at the end of the graves, ready to deliver his prepared speech. Though the king was as old as Aleam and the Council of Three, you wouldn't be able to see this just by looking at him. He did have grey hair, admittedly, but also his face looked remarkably free of wrinkles, and he had a set of brilliant white teeth. He had decided not to wear his crown today, perhaps as a reminder that we were all as mortal as each other.

"Our realm has now lost its magic," he said. "And it has also lost two of the bravest and most loyal fighters it has ever seen."

He went on to recount stories of both of their lives. Some of them brought smiles, and meows, and barks of agreement from those of us who could understand them. Others brought tears to human eyes, and caused sadness to well up in my heart that now understood human emotion far better than it had when I'd first entered this realm.

"These two brave souls still live on in our memories," King Garmin continued. "And it's those memories that we will cherish and they are the magic we still have within us. Such magic cannot be taken away from us. So today let us grieve, and let us also grieve tomorrow if we must. Because one day, we will rise stronger because they are still within us. And we shall carry them forever onwards until that moment it becomes time for us to rest in our own graves."

King Garmin took a deep breath to signal the end of his speech. His lips curled into a warm and understanding smile and his gaze passed over the crowd in front of him.

I saw it all in that moment – every single interaction of companionship, as if it all happened in slow motion. Asinda wiped her face with her handkerchief. Seramina rested her head on Ange's shoulder. Rine squeezed Bellari's hand. Max whimpered from his position curled up at Seramina's feet, and I wasn't the only cat who emitted a sad and poignant meow.

Then, after the king had taken one more heady breath, he nodded to Calin and then Larmend in turn. Together, they dug their shovels into the dirt and they passed the first clumps of soil into the graves.

EPILOGUE

I said at the beginning of all of this that my story didn't start in the hills of South Wales, where I'd once had a good life dashing through the long summer grass chasing butterflies.

Alas, with the death of magic, there also went my opportunity to go back there. But that didn't mean I couldn't have a good life once again.

Of course I missed my old master and mistress, together with their son from South Wales. But no doubt they would have adopted another cat in my absence – hopefully a stray like one of the street cats in Cimlean City. That cat, be it a tom or she-cat, would no doubt have had many good breakfasts of smoked salmon and milk from my bowl. And I'm pretty sure that they managed to enjoy them without an evil warlock passing his hands through a magical portal and yanking them into another dimension.

Still, for me, it had turned out okay. For everyone it had, in fact, in the end.

Max, Ta'ra and I returned to complete our studies at Dragonsbond Academy. So did Rine, Ange, Bellari, Seramina, and the other Initiates still enrolled there.

We continued our lessons throughout the spring and summer, though any classes in magic had been erased from the syllabus. I no longer had the ability to cast it out of my staff, and I also couldn't transform into a chimera. Luckily though, I hadn't lost the ability to speak the languages of all living creatures.

Admittedly, Ta'ra still could use her fairy magic, but she refused to do so. She told me she wanted to be a cat just like me, and that suited me just fine.

There was one benefit that came from not being able to use magic. That year, during the famous Sports Day, no students had an opportunity to use their magic to augment their positions in the competition.

Suffice it to say, Salanraja and I won the dragon egg-and-spoon-race that year. She won a trophy that she could forever display in her chamber, and I got a whole leg of turkey all to myself.

Alas, there hadn't been enough room to accept the rest of the dragon riding cats into Dragonsbond Academy. Instead, Matharon volunteered to take them through training exercises, with Esme as their teacher.

There was also no need for the White Guard anymore, and the unicorns were too revered – and too proud for that matter – to be used as regular horses. The unicorns could still use magic, but they refused to do so. They had apparently agreed among themselves that it was too sacred to be touched by humans, cats, or dogs. So they returned to the forest and after a while an air of mystery surrounded them.

After all, no one ever seemed to encounter them anymore, and we all began to wonder who these mystical creatures who had once protected Cimlean City from the wiles of *Cana Dei* had been. Whenever I heard humans discussing them, I had decided not to point out that whatever they were, they still smelled like regular horses.

It turned out that unicorn souls didn't link to their riders' souls in the Fifth Dimension in the same way as dragon souls linked to their riders'. A few White Mages had told me that unicorns never felt particularly sentimental about staying with their riders, and had always seen themselves as the boss. You see now why I'd never trusted them? They were nothing like dragons at all.

Of course, the White Mages who had once ridden them missed their work with animals. So instead they set up a massive mansion, big enough to hold them and all the street cats of Cimlean City. As far as I'm aware they all had a good life there, although I only really went to visit them a few times.

Yet, the King's Dragon Guard didn't die. Illumine Kingdom still needed it protectors, as a new threat had arisen in the Darklands. It turned out that the warlocks and their magical creations had divided Illumine Kingdom from a horde of barbarian invaders who inhabited the lands to the south and wielded a new type of magic that nobody had ever seen before. As soon as they learned the warlocks' former home was empty, they took the opportunity to swarm in, creating a need for King Garmin to reinforce the borders.

But they are a story for another day, and I have many more stories to tell.

For those who are wondering, though, I did end up getting my cottage in the countryside. My position in the King's Dragon Guard came along with a regular wage, and being a cat I didn't have the regular expenses that humans did. Instead, I spent my days riding Salanraja over rolling fields, and nights curled up in our Cimlean City residence with Ta'ra.

So Ta'ra and I saved our wages together, and we eventually could afford the large four-bedroomed thatched cottage of my dreams, not far from Colie Town. It was built on a farm, with plenty of adjacent fields. This meant that we had plenty of room for dragon and feline visitors.

Admittedly we only used it as a holiday home, and after the five years since I'd graduated from Dragonsbond Academy, Salanraja and I decided to throw a huge reunion party. We invited everyone we could think of, including everyone I'd met at Dragonsbond Academy and all the cats, not to mention Max.

It was a warm summer's day, the hot wind coming from the south. Visitors arrived in dribs and drabs throughout the day, everyone delighted to see their old friends again. That night, the humans and the dragons set up a campfire, so we could all sit around it and reminisce upon memories past. Mutton sausages were roasted upon the flames, and the smell of their juices elicited many smiles and purrs.

By now, Bellari and Rine were married, and Bellari was soon expecting the arrival of her first child. She had managed to completely rid herself of her dander allergies, and the cats flocked around her.

Asinda had also married Calin, and they already had a two-year old boy of their own whom they had decided to name Lars. Ange had also brought a female *companion* with her, a woman of her own age called Belle with long silver hair, like Seramina's but more wavy. Palimali still kept close to Ange's side like a loyal guardian. The desert cheetah had adapted well to this realm. Seramina didn't bring any partners, but she told us that she had started to take an interest in a young blacksmith who worked a forge near her residence in Cimlean City. She instead arrived alongside Aleam, having lost that shy teenage look and exuding confidence like the version of her we'd met in the Third Dimension. Aleam himself hadn't seemed to age in his elder years. I guess that was because he was getting really, really old.

Max didn't bring any *companions* with him either. He seemed more interested in the food than any of the cats were, watching it eagerly, his tongue hanging low beneath his chin.

Esme and Rex had also recently had kittens of their own. Funnily enough, none of Rex's genes had seemed to pass on to the litter. Instead all five of them looked like tiny versions of Esme, with bright blue eyes, shiny pink noses, and brilliant alabaster fur.

The little boy Lars had Asinda's agility. As we all sat on logs watching the flames, he ran happily chasing the kittens around the campfire. They all looked as if they were having a jolly good time.

While we talked, and ate, and the humans drank mead, the dragons kept to themselves sharing conversations telepathically inside their minds.

Salanraja had recently laid an egg of her own, although she never seemed ready to tell me who the father was. We kept the egg in a stable at the back of the cottage on a pile of hay, and we'd already taken a couple of month's leave as this was due to hatch. Ta'ra and Kada had also taken leave to stay with us during this time.

The evening rolled in, and I ate so much mutton sausage that I didn't think I'd be able to walk again. Ta'ra sat right next to me, also with a plate full of food in front of her. By that point, she had fallen fast asleep.

It was at that moment that I caught sight of one of Esme's kittens. She had detached herself from her meal and her siblings, and instead was heading straight towards the stable. I pulled myself up and managed to drag myself after her, despite my heavy tummy.

"*Where's it going?*" Salanraja asked inside my mind, and I could see her yellow eyes watching her through the darkness. "*Please don't tell me this kitten is a threat to my dragonet.*"

"*Really, what's it going to do?*" I asked. "*It's even smaller than Rex.*"

"*Just check it out, will you?*"

"*What do you think I'm doing?*"

A full moon hung in the sky, its light cutting through the night and blanketed on either side by two silver lined clouds. There was a coolness in the air now, and the smoke coming off the fire still smelled absolutely delicious.

The moonlight coming through the stable doorway framed the dragon egg perfectly. Its red scales seemed to sparkle in its light. It was twice my size. The kitten stalked up to it. She was the young she-cat that Esme and Rex had named Marble.

"What are you doing?" I asked her.

Marble spun around, startled. Then she blinked at me. "Wait. You're the one Mama calls Dragoncat . . ."

"I am," I said, lowering my head, trying not to let the fame get to me. "Now tell me, what do you want with Salanraja's egg?"

"Can you not hear it?" she said. "It's been talking to me for a while now. He says it's time."

"Time for what?"

But she didn't need to answer, because there came a loud cracking sound from in front of me, startling me. It sounded like stone breaking, as the egg in front of us seemed to splinter apart. Pieces fell from it, then a white dragonet emerged, covered in some kind of transparent goo. It extended a tiny talon, then two spindly wings folded out from its back and curled inwards again. It had fiery yellow eyes just like Salanraja. They focused on the kitten in front of it.

"He's here," Marble said, and she sauntered forward with the same grace as her mother. The newly born dragonet leaned forward, and he pushed his muzzle to Marble's pink nose.

ACKNOWLEDGMENTS

I WANTED TO SAY THANK YOU to the usual team, including Tarryn Thomas for editing and proofreading, my family, particularly my parents for their continuing support and my dear wife Ola for reading early drafts and providing valuable input.

Also, thank you as always to my ARC team. I really appreciate all the work that you put in helping to promote my novels.

Finally, thank you to every single reader – I appreciate everything that you do to support authors and the world of literature at large.

To betray the empire or her dragon?

In the era of dragons, airships, and automatons, Pontopa faces a difficult choice: she could work for the king, liaising with merchant traders, for good money. But this would support his war against dragons, putting Pontopa's own dragon in danger.

Or she could exile to a land where grey dragons run amok. But the king is ruthless and disobeying his edict would risk her parents' lives. It will take a chance meeting with her favourite author for Pontopa to make up her mind. And she'll discover that her destiny is not as clear-cut as she first realised.

Because a rare few remain from an ancient lineage who can sing legions of dragons into battle. In a now endangered era, Pontopa might just be a Dragonseer.

AVAILABLE AT MAJOR RETAILERS

9 781915 886583